HAMPTONS SURPRISE

A BEACHCOMBER DREAMS NOVEL

NEVE COTTRELL

TROPIC TURTLE PRESS

CHAPTER ONE

AUNT JEAN DIED ON A THURSDAY.

Alice nearly let the call go to voicemail, but her mother rarely telephoned during business hours.

"I guess I should call Dad," Alice said. Jean had actually been her father's aunt, but the task of sharing bad news with their adult children still fell to Ruthie, even though the couple had been divorced for forty years.

"Your father's fine. The woman was ninety-eight. This was hardly unexpected."

"I know, but I thought she was still going strong." Not that Alice kept close tabs on her. She was too consumed with her own survival to pay much attention to anyone else's.

"You're talking to the wrong person about that." For reasons known only to the two headstrong women, her mother had fallen out with Aunt Jean about twenty years ago. The family had simply accepted the estrangement, unwilling to ask the tough questions. "The memorial service is scheduled for Saturday, so you'll come tomorrow after work and stay through the following weekend."

"If the service is on Saturday, then we'll just drive back to the city Sunday night," Alice said.

"What's the rush? The kids have off school for spring break next week. You can make a vacation out of it and spend some time with your family for a change."

Alice winced. Naturally, her mother had looked up the school calendar. Alice had been careful not to mention the break in their recent text exchanges. The internet was both a blessing and a curse.

"I'm not retired like you, Mom. I have to work."

"What else is new?" her mother asked. "Life is about more than punching a clock, you know. Tell the firm you're working remotely."

"I don't think people punch clocks anymore."

"Not the point."

"Where's the service?" Alice asked in an effort to change the subject.

"Do you really need to ask? It's at the Beachcomber. She planned the whole thing in advance. Honestly, it's the most considerate thing she's ever done. I guess that's how you entertain yourself when you're nearing one hundred."

Beachcomber Winery was the estate Jean Hughes had owned since 1980. The land in Southampton had been in the Hughes family for generations, serving as a farm for most of that time, until the modern world demanded change. Aunt Jean had taken a huge risk when she decided to follow the path of the Hargraves, who first planted grapes on the North Fork in 1973. Local friends thought the venture wouldn't last more than a couple years. According to Alice's father, Hunton Hughes, it was the only risk his aunt had ever taken. Aunt Jean apparently disliked change in general, but when faced with the choice between selling the family land or using it for something else, she chose the latter. After much research and deliberation, she opted to plant grapes and, thus, the Beachcomber was born.

Alice hadn't been to the winery in years. In fact, she was pretty sure the last time she'd been there was for her own baby shower. Guests had been thrilled to attend a baby shower that revolved around wine. After all, only the guest of honor couldn't drink. She still wasn't sure how that had happened, given her mother's rift with Aunt Jean. Alice suspected her stepmom and sisters had been instrumental in selecting the venue and outvoting her mother.

"The Beachcomber makes sense," Alice said.

She had fond memories of playing hide-and-seek in the vineyard with her four younger siblings. The estate wasn't busy in the early days, giving the children the freedom to run amok. It reminded Alice of a biergarten, where the adults sat outside and drank, and the children entertained each other with imaginative games.

"Apparently, Penny's sixtieth birthday party was there," her mother said with the expected amount of derision. There was no love lost between Alice's mother and stepmother. "As far as I know, that was the last family gathering at the Beachcomber."

Alice vaguely recalled the invitation. Once her husband was diagnosed with pancreatic cancer, Alice avoided any alcohol-centered social events in solidarity. Greg died three years ago and Alice still found herself in the habit of not drinking—or socializing.

"Stay the week," her mother pressed. "I deserve time with my grandchildren."

"Then come to the city. You can hang out with them all week while I'm at the office." Alice secretly hoped her mother wouldn't take the bait. The apartment wasn't big enough for the three of them plus her mother's personality.

"You need to unchain yourself from that desk and live a little," her mother said, unrelenting.

"I'm a widow raising two teenagers in New York City. I don't have the luxury."

"Youth is wasted on the young," her mother grumbled. "I bet you haven't downloaded that app yet."

Alice closed her eyes and feigned ignorance. "What app?"

"The dating app I told you about. Maybe you can arrange to meet someone for coffee while you're here. Of course, that will be easier if you stay the whole week."

And then Alice would meet someone local and move back to her old stomping grounds with the kids. Alice knew what her mother's ideal world looked like—all three of her adult children within five miles of her. Chelsea and Finn were already there, leaving Alice as the lone holdout and the target of her mother's frequent ideas.

"I will if you will," Alice said, knowing what the response would be. Her mother had been single ever since the divorce and, as far as Alice knew, wholly inactive on the dating front.

Her mother laughed. "Nice try. I'm over seventy. The only men who are interested in seeing me naked have medical degrees."

This conversation was the reason Alice tended to let her mother's calls go to voicemail.

"I hate to cut this short, but I need to go to a department meeting now," she lied.

Her mother made a dismissive noise. "Fine. See you tomorrow night. Don't eat on the way. I'll make dinner."

"Please don't go to any trouble. It's Friday. I doubt we'll get there until late."

"It's Friday in March. Traffic won't be a problem. Bye now."

Alice hung up the phone and sighed. The memorial service

aside, the entire weekend would be spent dodging her mother's attempts to get them to stay the week. Arguably, Alice could work remotely from the Hamptons; she simply didn't want to. Aunt Jean's death would bring the whole family together—an unsettling prospect. Her parents' divorce may have occurred forty years ago, but the repercussions were still felt today. Alice had learned it was best to avoid the entirety of Long Island altogether. Greg was from New Jersey, which gave Alice an excuse to opt out of the Hamptons for most holidays. Following Greg's death, Alice continued the practice so her two children could maintain their bond with Greg's parents.

Lily and Martin Warren had been high school sweethearts and were still happily married. Initially, Alice had been suspicious of their relationship. She'd been certain that Greg was myopic when it came to his own family and simply failed to see the cracks. It was only after a few years of visiting them that Alice realized Lily and Martin genuinely adored each other. The idea had been so foreign to her that she didn't believe it was possible. Although her father had remarried and had two more children with Penny, their relationship had struck Alice as more a matter of convenience. After the divorce, her father had to care for three young children on his own half the time and he wanted a woman to help him. Penny happened to be in the right place at the right time—specifically, the tennis court where Hunton played. Penny was his younger, hotter tennis instructor and, a year later, she became his wife.

Alice understood the attraction on her father's side. Penny was petite and blonde and probably took years off his life in a good way. She was less certain what Penny's motivation was. It seemed impractical to marry an older man, knowing he would likely die so much sooner. Of course, the thought made Alice feel like a hypocrite since Greg didn't even make it to forty-five—a stark reminder that there were no guarantees in life.

A text from her son interrupted her thoughts. *Can I hang out with Josh and Julia Sat night?*

Sorry, we have to go to the Hamptons. She'd explain later. She hated sending important information via text.

Keegan responded with a laughing emoji. *I bet we're the only people who'd make it sound like a chore.*

Although he was only sixteen, he'd matured in leaps and bounds since Greg's death. By necessity, Alice assumed. He'd certainly shown he was clever enough to see through her smiles and platitudes.

We'll leave tomorrow after school.

Keegan responded with a vomiting emoji. Okay, so maybe 'matured' wasn't exactly the right word.

Alice immediately began typing a list on her phone of everything she'd need to pack. She remembered the unopened bottle of Xanax the doctor had prescribed after Greg's death but decided not to include it. She could survive a couple days in her family's presence. After all, she'd endured much, much worse.

CHAPTER TWO

"What do you think of chintz? I hear it's making a comeback."

Isabel Hughes made a choking sound. Brianna Carter was one of her best clients and the two had an excellent rapport, so Isabel didn't bother to sugarcoat her reaction.

Brianna laughed. "I take that as a no."

Isabel eyed the gleaming white walls and sleek furniture of Brianna's Upper East Side apartment. "Chintz isn't you, that's all."

Brianna folded her arms and regarded the interior. "No, you're absolutely right. I don't know what I was thinking."

"If you're rethinking the current design," Isabel began, "I'm sure we can come up with something more in keeping with your taste." Isabel knew Brianna's preferences better than anyone. She'd worked for her on multiple projects, including this very room three years ago.

Brianna toyed with her pearl necklace. "To be honest, I'm not sure I want to redo this room. It's just that we had friends visiting from England recently, and Charlotte mentioned how lovely this room would look with a bit of chintz."

One of the downsides of working for Brianna was that she had a tendency to be easily swayed by people she liked. Charlotte from England probably lived in a two-hundred-year-old house with the same chintz curtains and upholstery that had been chosen by her grandmother.

"I think you'd hate it within two months," Isabel said truthfully.

That seemed to settle the matter. "You always set me straight. It's one of the reasons I love working with you."

"If your heart was truly set on chintz, you know I wouldn't stand in your way."

Brianna sighed. "I think my heart was truly set on Charlotte's approval, but cooler heads have prevailed." She smiled. "Listen, I know it's short notice, but I'm having a little get-together tomorrow evening. You should come. A couple of your other clients will be here—Missy Tinsdale and Talia Morgenstern."

Isabel maintained a neutral expression. She didn't particularly like either woman, although their interior design projects were plentiful and paid well. Missy referred to Isabel as 'Bel,' despite Isabel's repeated corrections. She'd also witnessed two of Missy's infamous temper tantrums, one of which was directed at Isabel after she'd ordered a light gray sofa instead of a white one. Talia wasn't any better. Isabel had once heard her describe a friend's breast cancer as a blessing because it meant she had an excuse to fix her lopsided boobs. If the friend had been present, it would've been possible Talia was trying to make her feel better. As it happened, the friend wasn't there and the cackle of laughter that punctuated the remark told Isabel everything she needed to know about Talia Morgenstern.

"I'd love to," Isabel lied, "but I'm going to the Hamptons this weekend."

Brianna frowned. "In March?"

"I'm not going for pleasure. I have to attend a memorial service for my father's aunt."

"I didn't realize you had family out there."

"Most of my family lives there. It's where I grew up."

Brianna gave her a long look. "How did I not know that about you? I just assumed you grew up in Manhattan."

Isabel shrugged. "I moved here for college and have lived here ever since."

Brianna's face brightened. "You know what? You should take a look at our beach house while you're there. I've been considering redoing the pool house and I'd love your thoughts. I don't think we've changed so much as a throw pillow in years."

Isabel suspected that Brianna's pool house was likely twice the size of Isabel's apartment. "Any idea of the square footage?"

"About two thousand square feet. My brother's been staying in the main house while his place is being renovated. He can let you in."

Isabel licked her lips. "I appreciate the offer, but I'm not really sure I can fit it in. I'm coming back Sunday night."

Brianna flicked a bejeweled finger. "Nonsense. If you're going all the way out there, stay an extra couple days and see your family. Ooh, and if you're in Sag Harbor, swing by Cavaniola's and bring me back a couple of their gift baskets. Their cheese is to die for."

Isabel debated the offer. Jackson had agreed to accompany her, but maybe it would be better if she stayed behind in the Hamptons and he returned to their apartment. It would give them the time apart that Isabel desperately craved.

"If you're sure…"

"Of course I'm sure. You're the only one I trust, Isabel. You know that."

Isabel felt an unexpected sense of relief at the prospect of spending time away from her life. "Then I'd be happy to."

Brianna beamed. "Great. I'll text Mason and let him know you're coming."

CHAPTER THREE

"Two hours in a car?" Keegan pressed his forehead against the passenger window.

"I like a long car ride," Amelia chirped from the back seat. She was always willing to be contrary, especially in response to her brother's opinion.

Alice still couldn't believe she was the mother of two teenagers. Where did the time go? One minute, she was near death in childbirth. The next minute, she was driving along the expressway, listening to them bicker about which YouTube personality had more subscribers.

She glanced at Amelia in the rearview mirror. With her light brown hair and bright blue eyes, her daughter strongly resembled Greg, whereas Keegan was the perfect blend of both parents. He'd inherited Alice's dark hair and gray eyes, and his father's tall, stocky build. Amelia was tall, too, although not stocky, and Alice wondered whether it was only a matter of time before genetics caught up to her. She was only thirteen and the hormones had only just begun to wreak havoc on the girl's system. Alice prayed to the universe for mercy on that front.

"Read a book," Alice said, and returned her focus to the road.

"You know I get car sick if I read." Keegan's tone was sulky and Alice steeled herself for additional protests, but thankfully none was forthcoming.

"You're not the only one," Amelia said.

Yes, Alice had been blessed with not one, but two children prone to car sickness. Good thing they lived in the city.

"Did I ever meet Aunt Jean?" Amelia asked.

"Once, not long after you were born."

"I think I remember."

Keegan twisted to glare at his sister. "You do not. Humans don't even form memories that early."

Amelia lifted her chin a fraction. "I did. I can remember being in my crib. I had a toy monkey and a farm animal mobile."

"That's only because you've seen the photos." Keegan faced front again, shaking his head. "She's such a liar."

Amelia responded with a swift kick to the back of his seat.

"That's enough of that," Alice said firmly. She focused on keeping an even tone and not raising her voice. It wasn't easy, but she was proud of herself for managing it.

"Why are we going out of our way to go to her memorial service if we didn't go out of our way to see her when she was alive?"

Sometimes Alice looked at her daughter and saw a pint-sized journalist, meting out the tough questions that no one else dared to ask.

"It's a sign of respect," Alice said. She didn't want to explain the feud between her mother and Aunt Jean, mostly because she couldn't.

Keegan slumped in the seat. "Can we stop somewhere to eat? I'm starving."

"Mom-mom is making dinner," she said.

The children groaned in unison and Alice bit back a smile. It seemed she'd passed on more than her genes.

"She boils all her vegetables," Keegan complained.

"To death," Amelia added. "They get so soggy. It's like eating a plant that was left out in the rain."

Alice kept her eyes on the road. "I'll let you leave the one-star review once we've left town."

"Can't we stay with Aunt Chelsea?" Amelia asked.

"Chelsea has a full house. Besides, it's only for the weekend."

Amelia grunted her disapproval. "Mom-mom always asks me if I brushed my hair right after I've done it."

Not to be outdone, Keegan added his own Mom-mom experience. "When we FaceTimed last month, I told her I got an A minus on my math test and she asked me what I screwed up."

Alice said nothing. She was familiar with her mother's parenting style. Ruthie Alpert could make it all the way to the Moon and only see the dark side.

"She keeps pestering me about boys, asking if I have a crush on anyone," Amelia continued. "It's annoying."

Alice hit the button for the radio to drown out the sounds of insubordination. She didn't want to hear any more complaints. They only served to reinforce her own opinion of the matter.

Keegan rolled his eyes. "Not old people music." He changed the station until he found a song he deemed more palatable. The moment he made his selection, an incoming call cut through the music.

Alice glanced at the screen and pressed her lips into a line. She recognized the number of one of the firm's most important clients and reluctantly accepted the call.

"Alice Hughes."

"Alice, it's Benjamin Barnes. I wanted to talk to you about that trademark search report."

"I would be happy to discuss the results with you, Mr. Barnes, but I'm driving right now. Can I call you back?" Alice was a multitasker in many areas of her life, but the car wasn't one of them. The older she got, the more she needed to focus on the road.

"As soon as you can, please. I'd like to check this off my list before the weekend." He hung up before Alice could respond.

"Doesn't he know the weekend already started?" Amelia asked.

"Not his, apparently." Alice was accustomed to clients who worked around the clock, which was one of the main reasons she, too, worked nonstop.

"Will Uncle Finn be there?" Keegan asked.

"Not sure if he'll be at dinner, but he'll be at the service tomorrow."

"And Pop-pop?" Amelia asked.

"Yes, he and Penny will definitely be there tomorrow."

Amelia fidgeted in the seat. "Why do we call your mother Mom-mom, but Penny is Penny?"

"Because Mom-mom is our real grandmother and Penny isn't," Keegan said, before Alice had a chance to answer.

"I don't like the word 'real,'" Alice said. "Penny is a lovely woman and she's been very good to us."

"We should give her a special name," Amelia said.

"You might've decided on that earlier in life," Keegan said.

"It's not my fault," Amelia protested.

The truth was that Alice had avoided choosing a special name for Penny because she knew it would upset her mother and Chelsea had followed suit when she had kids. So Penny stayed Penny.

"If you're serious, I would suggest brainstorming now

rather than at Mom-mom's," Alice said. She could only imagine the names her mother would put forth, most of them inappropriate for children.

"I think Penny prefers her own name," Keegan said.

"How do you know? Aunt Isabel and Uncle Freddie don't have any kids of their own yet." She poked her head between the head rests and looked at Alice. "Do you think one of them will have kids soon?"

"I have no idea," Alice said.

"I hope so," Amelia said. "Then we'd actually get to see our cousins because they live in the city."

Alice felt a pang of guilt. Chelsea and Brendan lived in the Hamptons, so Amelia and Keegan rarely saw their three cousins, except on FaceTime.

"Can we go see the lighthouse?" Amelia asked.

Keegan craned his neck to give his sister an incredulous look. "That's like another hour from Mom-mom's."

"Are you sure? I don't remember it being that far."

Alice glanced at her daughter in the rearview mirror. "Really? Because the last time we went, you complained you were carsick for most of the journey." The historic Montauk Point Light was on Turtle Hill at the far end of the island. It was a popular spot for visitors, and Alice had made a point of showing it off to Greg during their first trip to the Hamptons together. He liked Montauk so much that he made it essential viewing every time they returned. Apparently, his enthusiasm had rubbed off on Amelia.

"I don't remember that," Amelia said. "I just like the lighthouse." She turned to gaze out her window, offering Alice a view of her perfect profile. Amelia had inherited Greg's sloped nose, for which Alice was grateful. Alice's nose had 'character,' according to her mother, but Alice didn't believe that any body part should be described that way.

"You know I love Montauk, too, but we won't have time.

This is a quick trip, remember?" Alice hated to say no, knowing that a visit to the lighthouse would be a way for Amelia to feel connected to her dad. But still. They were only here for a short stay and there were plenty of memories in the city. After all, that had been their home as a family. Not here. Never here.

Keegan took control of the radio again and Alice sank into a dream state as she drove along Montauk Highway. When she saw a sign for Westhampton, Alice's tension returned anew.

Not far now.

CHAPTER FOUR

RUTHIE ALPERT HUGHES wiped her hands on a dishcloth and adjusted the hem of her top. Her oldest child was only ten minutes away and Ruthie wanted to make sure dinner was ready the moment they arrived.

Finn hovered in the doorway to the kitchen. Once he heard Alice was coming tonight, he insisted on coming over to see his sister. "Should I open the wine?"

"I thought you were having beer," Ruthie said.

"That was my pre-dinner drink. I'm thinking ahead."

Ruthie smiled at her only son. It was such a Finn thing to say. "White or red?"

"You made lasagna, right? I think the answer's obvious."

Ruth inclined her head. "In the pantry."

Finn entered the walk-in pantry and emerged with a bottle, chuckling. "Still won't buy any Beachcomber, huh?"

Ruthie's expression soured. "I'm sure we'll have plenty of it tomorrow," she said. Ruthie wasn't exactly happy about Aunt Jean's passing, but she wasn't unhappy either. The woman had lived a long and prosperous life to the ripe old age of ninety-eight. As far as lives and deaths went, Aunt Jean was more fortunate than most.

"No one's forcing you to go, you know," Finn said.

Ruthie glared at him. "I'm going. It isn't like she'll be there."

Finn's eyes twinkled with mischief. "You never know. She might be there in spirit."

"And what? I'll burst into flames upon arrival like a vampire in church?"

Even though Jean was Hunton's aunt and no blood relation of Ruthie's, the older woman hadn't taken sides during the divorce. Their rift occurred years later, a fact which Ruthie was unable to forgive. She'd loved Aunt Jean like she was her own flesh and blood, and it had come as a terrible shock to learn there were limits to Aunt Jean's love. Ruthie had believed it was unconditional and the discovery that it wasn't had hardened her heart that little bit more.

"I haven't been to the Beachcomber in forever," Finn said. "I don't even know anyone who's been there recently. It isn't a place that comes up in conversation."

Finn would know. As a realtor, Ruthie knew he kept abreast of all the local business chatter.

"Maybe it's fallen on hard times," Ruthie said.

Finn gave her a pointed look. "Try not to sound so pleased."

Jessica entered the kitchen and Ruthie's eyes were immediately drawn to her daughter-in-law's trim waist. It wouldn't kill her to eat more calories and cut down on hours at the gym. She was starting to look emaciated.

"Can I help with anything?" Jessica asked. As far as daughters-in-law went, Jessica was decent. Not quite up to Ruthie's standards for her only son, but it could've been worse. Finn could've married Georgina, the one before Jessica. Ruthie never would've gotten over it. Georgina was one of those women with more ideas than sense. She marched in protests and didn't wear a bra half the time. Ruthie couldn't understand what Finn saw in her, other than the convenience of no bra. She'd been relieved when they'd called it quits. Apparently, Finn was 'too much of a capitalist' because he sold houses in the Hamptons. It was ironic, really. Ruthie still remembered Finn as a teenager who resented that girls were more interested in the rich kids who swarmed the beaches and parties in July and August. Of course, those wealthy teens were now adults who bought their own luxury properties in the Hamptons, courtesy of Hughes Realty.

A fellow realtor, Jessica was more his speed, although Ruthie wondered why they were waiting so long to start a family. Finn was forty-two and Jessica was thirty-seven. Tick tock, she thought. Time waits for no man or woman. She knew this fact all too well.

"I think we're ready," Ruthie said. "I tried not to overcook the broccoli." Her cooking was the target of criticism and Alice came to stay so infrequently that Ruthie didn't want to give her or the kids any reason to complain.

"The table's set," Jessica said.

"Thank you. Would you open that bottle, Finn? I think I'd like a drink now."

"It's a shame Chelsea and Brendan couldn't be here," Jessica said.

"I know, but one of the kids has an activity of some kind," Ruthie said. There were so many commitments between those three kids that she couldn't keep up with them.

"They're coming to the memorial service tomorrow, right?" Finn asked.

"Oh, yes." She turned away from the oven. "I suppose your father and Penny will be there, too."

Finn handed her a glass of wine. "I should think so. Jean was his aunt."

"You don't need to remind me."

"I'm looking forward to seeing Freddie and Isabel, too," Finn said. "They're as bad as Alice when it comes to visiting."

"They're young," Ruthie said. "The city's a more exciting place to be at that age."

"Not to me," Finn said.

No. Ruthie knew early on that Finn wouldn't be a city boy. Even the occasional trip to Manhattan to see a show or go to a museum made her son twitchy. Like her, he disliked the hustle and bustle and the crowded spaces. He was much happier in the Hamptons, especially during the off-season when locals had the run of the place.

The slamming of a car door interrupted her thoughts. "They're here."

Finn went to the door to greet his sister. He hadn't seen Alice or her kids in six months. He and Jessica had gone into the city for a weekend to see a show and they'd had dinner at Alice's apartment afterward. He felt guilty for not seeing her more frequently since Greg died, but his work kept him busy. Jessica had suggested inviting them to visit more than once, and Finn had given a noncommittal response. He knew his sister wasn't keen on making the trek to the Hamptons. Finn was aware of Alice's efforts to circumnavigate their mother and he didn't blame her. Ruthie could be difficult, as all mothers could. Jessica's parents lived in Florida now, so most of their time was spent in the company of Finn's divided family.

He opened the front door and waved. Alice had already unzipped her coat and Finn immediately conjured up a memory of their last dinner conversation. Alice had complained of hot flashes and insomnia and they'd laughed at Finn's apparent discomfort. He'd changed the subject to the Mets, which only prompted more laughter. He was glad Jessica wasn't there yet. He didn't want to hear about menopause. He barely wanted to hear about her menstrual cycle, but he didn't have much of choice given how much importance it had in their lives right now.

"Hello, brother." Alice slipped off her coat and hung it on the rack in the foyer.

Finn balked at the sight of his niece and nephew. It had only been six months, yet they each seemed to have sprouted another couple inches.

"Hey, Uncle Finn," Keegan said, a little too loudly.

Finn noticed the wireless earbuds and tapped one. "You might want to take those off before your grandmother sees them." No electronics at the table, that was the rule. Finn wasn't even permitted to take a work call during mealtimes. Dinner at his mother's house made him feel like a child again, and not in a good way.

"It's not like we're eating yet." Despite the protest, Keegan tugged the earbuds from his ears.

"Wine," Alice blurted.

Finn suppressed a smile. Alcohol was a necessity when it came to enduring dinner conversation with their mother. Half the time it was more akin to an interrogation. Alice got the brunt of it, of course. That was the price she paid for leaving the Hamptons and for letting their mother's calls go to voicemail more often than not.

"Ask and you shall receive," Jessica said. She tapped the counter where a glass of wine was ready and waiting.

Alice cradled the glass in both hands like she was about to drink water she'd sourced from the Fountain of Youth. "This is the only glass I'm having or I won't be able to function tomorrow."

"Still out of practice?" Finn asked.

Alice nodded before taking a hesitant sip.

"How were the roads?" Ruthie asked.

"They were fine, Mom-mom." Amelia bounded over to hug her grandmother. She reminded Finn of an eager Labrador. She seemed far too upbeat for a teenager, especially one who'd lost her dad to cancer. Finn would've been a brooding mess. He was only two when his parents divorced, so he'd been spared the memories of an intact family. Even with that mercy, he'd been a moody teenager.

"When's the last time you had a haircut?" Ruthie asked, gently pulling a strand of Amelia's long hair.

Amelia ducked her head and took a step backward. Inwardly, Finn sighed. Could his mother not see how her words affected others? She'd been the same with all of them— no one was immune to Ruthie's criticisms-disguised-as-concern. When he had a child of his own, he would make sure his mother gave more thought to the things she said. When he'd said this to Jessica once, she'd laughed until she choked.

"She's growing it out," Alice said. "Then she wants to cut it for Locks of Love."

His mother scowled. "I never liked the idea of someone else wearing my hair. It's odd."

"You say that because you have a full head of hair," Keegan said. "You might feel differently if you were bald from chemo."

Finn raised his eyebrows at Alice but said nothing. He was impressed with his nephew, pushing back without sounding like a complete twat. Good for him.

"Dinner's ready," his mother announced. "Why don't we eat before it gets cold? I have it on good authority that nobody likes cold broccoli."

They moved to the dining table and Finn waited dutifully until his mother told them where to sit. He knew better than to try and take any seat he wanted.

"That creepy portrait's still here," he heard Amelia whisper to her brother.

"It was here when Mom was little. I don't think it has plans to go anywhere," Keegan whispered back.

Finn snorted. The portrait hung on the living room wall, which was, thankfully, the least-used room in the house. 'Fat Baby,' as the portrait was known in their family, depicted a child of an uncertain age wearing a white frilly hat and dress. His mother had purchased it from a local antiques dealer when he was a kid during her Colonial Williamsburg phase. One summer his mother had driven the three kids to Virginia and she'd become intent on recreating the look of the historic homes they'd viewed there. The living room acquired floral prints, a pineapple lamp, and Fat Baby. It wasn't an attractive painting and the eyes followed you around the room. It was strangely reassuring to know their rejection of the portrait had been passed down to the next generation.

"What are your friends doing over spring break?" Finn asked the kids.

"I bet they're not all going somewhere as wonderful as the Hamptons," his mother interjected.

"My friend Diego is going to Puerto Rico with his family," Keegan said.

"Lucy's gone to Miami," Amelia said. "Her family has a condo right on the water."

"We have miles of beaches right here," his mother said, cutting her lasagna into small squares.

"But it's cold now," Amelia said. "Miami is hot."

"Miami also has a lot of drugs," his mother said.

Finn slapped his forehead. "Mom, let's not..."

"That reminds me," his mother said, "I need to call the doctor for a new prescription. I've had this UTI for weeks. If these antibiotics don't get rid of it, I'll need a bladder transplant."

"I don't think that's a thing," Keegan said.

"Of course it is," his mother said. "If they can clone a goat from DNA, they can transplant a bladder."

Amelia frowned. "You need surgery?"

"Mom-mom's exaggerating," Alice said. "Nobody needs surgery."

"I'm not sure that we need to hear about your medical issues over dinner," Finn said.

"Well, when else would you hear about them?" his mother demanded. "This is the only time I have a captive audience."

"Let's change the subject," Jessica said. "This lasagna is delicious, Ruth."

"I'll give you the recipe, that way you can make it for your own kids when you finally get around to having them."

Finn's stomach tightened. This was not the direction he wanted the conversation to go. Before he could intervene, he caught a whiff of a strange scent and sniffed the air. "What's that smell?" It reminded him of burnt toast.

His mother's brow creased. "I don't know." Her gaze traveled over the table. "All the food's been served and I'm pretty sure I turned off the oven."

'Pretty sure' didn't sound like sure enough to Finn. He pushed back his chair and went into the kitchen to see smoke billowing from the oven.

"Everyone outside," Finn directed. He grabbed the fire extinguisher from the cabinet under the sink and sprayed.

"I never should've made that joke about bursting into flames," his mother said, lingering in the doorway.

"What? You think Aunt Jean did this?" He would've laughed, but he was too busy putting out the fire.

"I called the fire department," Alice said, as calm and

composed as ever. He swore his sister had been born with Valium in her veins.

"We don't need the fire department," his mother said. "Finn took care of it."

Alice shrugged. "Too late now."

"They have to come and inspect it for safety reasons," Finn said. He knew more about fire safety codes than he cared to admit, thanks to his real estate business.

His mother stared forlornly at the oven. "You don't think I need a new oven, do you?"

"I doubt it," Finn said. But better safe than sorry.

"This is what I get for trying to cook a nice meal for my family," his mother said.

Finn glanced at the ceiling. "Why didn't the smoke alarm turn on?"

"I took the batteries out," his mother said. "It kept beeping in the middle of the night."

Finn wanted to smack her. "That's their way of telling you to replace the batteries!"

The sound of a siren alerted them to the arrival of a fire truck.

"Cool," Amelia said, her eyes wide.

The fire chief swept into the kitchen to inspect the damage.

"Sorry about this," Finn said to the older man.

"It happens." The fire chief turned to face them. "If you could clear the area, that would be helpful."

Finn ushered everyone into the living room because it was the farthest room from the kitchen. They settled onto the sectional sofa and all eyes drifted instinctively to the portrait on the wall. Fat Baby stared back at them, unblinking.

"Mom, can I sleep with you tonight?" Amelia asked, her hands clasped on her lap.

Alice responded without hesitation. "Sure."

The fire chief poked his head in. "All clear. Everything looks good. You were very lucky."

His mother barked a laugh. "Not something I hear very often."

"What caused the fire?" Alice asked.

"There was a piece of melted plastic at the bottom of the oven," the fire chief said. "We scraped it off for you, but can't tell you what it was."

His mother's face drained of color. "Oops. I think I know. I used a plastic fork earlier and it must've fallen in without me noticing."

A plastic fork.

Finn exhaled. It was always something.

"Thanks for coming." Finn escorted the fire chief to the door. "Hope we didn't pull you away from anything important."

"No worries," the chief replied.

Finn continued to stand in the open doorway and watched the glow of the red lights until they were swallowed by the darkness. Tomorrow the whole family would be together under the Beachcomber's roof. He really hoped tonight wasn't an omen of things to come.

CHAPTER FIVE

THE BEACHCOMBER HADN'T AGED a day, unlike Alice, who'd spotted new wrinkles at the corners of her mouth. If she participated in Lent, she would've given up mirrors.

A genuine smile passed her lips when she spotted the rest of her siblings, as well as her dad and Penny. Everyone was already in attendance, it seemed.

"Looks like Penny's gained a few pounds," her mother said. "That's what happens when you can't play tennis every day."

"I think she looks the same," Alice said.

"You would think she would've worn black. It's both respectful and slimming."

Alice turned toward her mother. "You'll behave yourself with Dad and Penny, won't you?"

"Don't be insulting. If they stay at their end of the table and I stay at mine, we'll be fine."

It *was* a large room, but it was also a room filled with tension and alcohol. It didn't help that Alice was still scarred by the events of her fortieth birthday party. Her mother and Greg had plotted together and, naturally, her father and

Penny had been included on the guest list. All the adults had overindulged on cocktails, with the exception of Chelsea. Her parents began arguing over which one of them refused to get a dog when they were married, and the evening spiraled out of control from there. Alice hid in the restroom of the restaurant until the bill had been paid and she could slink out the door unnoticed.

Greg later apologized profusely. He'd been too frightened of Ruthie to say no to the idea. If only they'd realized then that an unpleasant birthday party would be the least of their worries.

Alice crossed the room of the winery to greet her father and stepmother, who were engaged in conversation with an attractive, thirty-something man. She spotted the tastevin around his neck and realized he must be the sommelier. She didn't recall much about the winery, but she had definite memories of the shallow silver cup that the previous sommelier had worn on a chain around his neck. He'd once explained its purpose was to better judge the color and clarity of the wine when in a dimly lit room. Alice couldn't remember his name, but she remembered the tastevin.

"We make a selection of varietals…" the sommelier said.

"Wait, I thought you made wine," her father interrupted. "What's a varietal?"

"It's wine made primarily from a single variety of grape, such as Cabernet Franc, Cabernet Sauvignon, Chardonnay, Merlot and Pinot Noir."

Penny nudged him. "Don't test the poor guy, Hunton. You know this stuff."

"Just because I knew it years ago doesn't mean I remember," her father said. "That's what getting older does to you."

"I'm happy to answer any questions you have," the sommelier said. Alice thought he seemed unfailingly patient.

"How many calories in a case?" her father asked.

Penny patted his paunch. "Let's not find out, dear."

Her father's gaze finally landed on her. "There's my girl."

"Hi, Dad." Alice hugged him first and then turned to kiss Penny's cheek. "Hey, Penny."

"You're looking well," Penny said. "How's work?"

Alice offered a wan smile. "It's work."

"Alice!" Isabel rushed over to embrace her. Not for the first time, Alice was startled by how much Isabel resembled Penny, except for the blue hair, of course. Her younger sister's hair had been blue the last time they'd seen each other in the city, but Alice was surprised she hadn't chosen to tone it down for the memorial service.

"I'm so glad to see you," Alice said. "I wish we could've all ridden together."

"Not with our mixed schedules," Isabel said. "I couldn't ride with Freddie either." She nodded her head toward their brother, who was now talking to the sommelier.

"At least we're all here," Alice said. "Aunt Jean would've liked that."

Isabel spun toward Amelia and Keegan. "I swear you both grow an inch a month. I only saw you a few weeks ago and you're taller."

"Where's Jackson?" Keegan asked.

"Touring the cellar. He'll be back in a few minutes."

"Where are you staying tonight?" Alice asked.

"With Dad and Penny," Isabel said. "I'm staying in the Hamptons for a few days, but Jackson needs to get back."

Alice shot her a quizzical look. "You're not going back together?"

She shook her head. "I'm staying in town for work."

"In that case, he could've driven with us," Alice said. "Next time, we'll coordinate better." She felt foolish saying 'next time,' as though she anticipated more death-related family gatherings in their future.

For the next hour, Alice almost forgot she was there for a memorial service. She was too distracted playing military strategist and maneuvering between her parents whenever one migrated too close to the other one. It helped that the wine was flowing and the food was wonderful. A couple of positives to offset the negatives.

"Can Keegan and I see the vineyard?" Amelia asked.

Alice glanced at the thin material of her daughter's dress. "Yes, but wear your coat. It's cold."

"You know what? I wouldn't mind a walk outside," Isabel said.

Alarm bells rang in Alice's head as she noticed her mother inching toward her dad and Penny. "Mom, come outside with us!"

Isabel gave her arm a gentle squeeze. "Good idea."

A mini-exodus followed. Her mom took Keegan and Amelia on a guided tour, although Amelia quickly grew bored and returned to Alice and Isabel, just as Finn and Jessica made their way outside to join them.

"Smart move, keeping Mom occupied," Finn said.

Alice smiled. "Like riding a bicycle."

Isabel glanced inside the winery where the rest of the family remained rooted in place. "We should see if the other kids want to escape out here."

"Danny won't be allowed by himself," Amelia said. "He's too much of a handful."

Alice cringed, hearing her words parroted to someone else. In her defense, Alice had only been repeating something she'd heard from her own mother.

Isabel snickered. "He's an exuberant little boy, but I think he'll be fine with all these adults out here."

Amelia looked at her. "Do you think you'll have kids soon, Aunt Isabel?"

Isabel appeared so stricken that Alice wordlessly handed her the untouched glass of wine she'd been holding.

"It's hard to predict the future," Isabel said vaguely.

Alice was relieved that Jackson wasn't within earshot. So far, they'd gotten through the event without anyone asking Isabel or Jackson when they planned to get engaged.

Amelia turned to direct the same question to Finn and Jessica. "What about you, Aunt Jess? It would be fun to have a baby in the family again."

Jessica paled and glanced helplessly at her husband. Finn coiled an arm around her waist and squeezed.

"It seems like only yesterday that you were the baby in the family," Finn said.

Alice didn't miss the look of anguish in Jessica's eyes, nor did she miss the fact that neither answered the question. There was a story there, but Alice left it alone. She wasn't her mother; Finn and Jessica's issues were no business of hers.

Jackson finally joined them outside, and Alice thought he and Isabel seemed off. She'd thought that the last time she saw them together as well, yet they were obviously still a couple.

The sound of delicate chimes drifted through the air and drew Alice's attention inside. Her father stood at the head of the table, dangling a silver bell.

"I think that's our cue," Finn said.

Everyone returned to the table for the service itself, which was informal and brief. People were invited to say a few words about Jean. Alice spoke a few words, as did her father and Penny. Alice was relieved when her mother declined to speak. A wise decision.

· · ·

The moment the speeches finished, Jackson shot to his feet. "I'm sorry to leave you all, but I need to be heading back to the city."

"Tonight?" Penny asked.

Isabel knew she should've preempted his departure by telling everyone he'd be leaving early to avoid this reaction. She'd let everyone think he was staying the night.

Her father stood to shake Jackson's hand. "It's a shame you can't stay. We're about to open more wine." He gave Jackson a long look that suggested maybe he should rethink his plans.

Isabel felt compelled to jump to his defense. "Dad, he has to work and so do I. The only reason I'm staying longer is because my work is here for a change."

Jackson took the comment in stride. "Summer's around the corner, Mr. Hughes. Plenty of time for get-togethers."

Isabel didn't miss Jackson's strained smile. It was an appropriate look—everything about the two of them was strained right now.

"I hope so," her father said. "I'm not getting any younger. I want to spend quality time with my kids while I still have the use of my legs."

Isabel leaned into her father. "Don't say things like that. You're perfectly healthy."

He kissed the top of her head. "Only because my kids and grandkids are around to keep me young."

Isabel flinched at the mention of grandkids. She knew her family wondered…She knew that everyone wondered, really. Isabel was thirty-six. She had a career and a relationship. They believed it was time.

Isabel didn't have the heart to tell them the truth.

.   .   .

Alice watched in silence as Isabel escorted Jackson from the winery. Something was amiss there and she wondered whether anyone else had noticed.

Her mother's loud voice drew her attention back to the table. She should've cut her off an hour ago, really, but she'd been too preoccupied catching up with everyone.

"You know," her mother said, to no one in particular. "The Beachcomber has a very special place in our hearts and not just because of Jean. It's also where Hunton and I came to celebrate our divorce when this place was still shiny and new." She batted her thick eyelashes at her ex-husband. "We asked for the most expensive bottle of wine on the menu and the sommelier assumed we were here for an anniversary."

"I remember Hunton telling me about that," Penny said. "I thought it was a nice thing to do. After all, you had three children to raise together, regardless of your marital status."

"So glad you approve," her mother said, in a way that suggested she didn't give a flying fig about Penny's opinion.

"Speaking of expensive bottles," Finn said, angling his head toward a bottle on the table. "Baz brought this out a little bit ago. He said Aunt Jean specifically asked that we drink this in her memory."

Her father reached for the bottle. "Excellent."

"I think we should wait for Baz," Alice said. If Aunt Jean had instructed the sommelier to serve this wine, it seemed only right to let him do it.

"No need to wait," her father said, rising to his feet. "I can manage it."

"Please don't strain yourself," Penny said, her voice barely above a whisper.

Her father narrowed his eyes. "It's a wine cork, not Excalibur." As he struggled to liberate the cork, his face grew flushed.

"If you can't do it, there's no shame in admitting it,"

Ruthie said, although it was clear she enjoyed watching his wrestling match.

He placed the bottle between his knees for a better grip and—success! The cork popped out, but he quickly lost control. Wine erupted from the bottle and splashed all over the woman hurrying over to assist him—his ex-wife.

Alice watched in horror as her mother rushed straight into a shower of red wine. She stopped short, her face and chest dripping, and there was a collective gasp as everyone awaited Ruthie's reaction.

"Well, that was unfortunate," her mother said. She swiped a cloth napkin from the table and wiped her face. "Good thing I'm wearing black."

Alice saw the look of disbelief in her father's eyes and knew exactly what he was thinking—who was this agreeable woman and what had she done with his ex-wife?

"I'm so sorry, Ruthie," he said. "It was an accident, truly."

"Oh, I know. You're as clumsy as ever."

Ah, there was the woman her father remembered.

Alice scraped back her chair and stood. "Come on, Mom. Let's get you cleaned up in the restroom."

Alice guided her to the back of the winery.

"That's my punishment for trying to be helpful," her mother said. She rinsed off the droplets in the sink and fixed her hair.

"You do know it was an accident."

"I do, and that's why I'm keeping my composure. Besides, it was a little bit funny." Her mother smiled at her reflection in the mirror.

"You're drunk," Alice said. It was the only explanation.

"Not the first I've been drunk at the Beachcomber. There was this one time not long after my divorce…"

Alice closed her eyes and wished herself onto a Caribbean beach. "I don't need to hear the gory details, thanks."

Her mother patted her cheek. "How did I raise such a prude? Some mothers worry about their daughters getting pregnant. I worried you'd never…"

Alice clamped a hand over her mother's mouth. "Let's rejoin the others and find a new topic of conversation." In fact, she was more than ready to leave. She planned to say her goodbyes and head out.

Her immediate plan was thwarted, however, by the arrival of a silver-haired man in a business suit. As he strode toward their table, Alice thought he looked vaguely familiar, but she couldn't quite place him.

Her father stood to shake the man's hand. "Hello, Jeffrey. I didn't realize you were coming."

"Jean gave me specific instructions, so here I am." The man surveyed the seating options. "Is there a place for me?"

Her father vacated his chair at the head of the table and Finn jumped up to borrow one from a neighboring table for his father.

"For those of you who don't know me, I'm Jeffrey Sturgeon, Jean's lawyer, and I'm here to share some news about her estate."

Ah, that was why Alice recognized him. Sturgeon & Associates handled her father's affairs as well.

"Shouldn't there be a formal reading of the will?" Penny asked.

Jeffrey opened his briefcase and produced a document. "This is the way Jean asked me to handle it. Obviously, her most important asset is this establishment." He glanced around the winery. "She didn't want to disrupt the business…"

"Are we really doing this now?" her mother interrupted. "At a memorial service? I would think we could at least wait until the dirt settled."

"She's being cremated," Penny pointed out.

Her mother bristled. "I know that. It's only a figure of speech."

Jeffrey cleared his throat. "This was my client's request. She thought it was perhaps the only time you'd all agree to be in the same room together."

A guilty silence followed.

"I'll cut to the chase so you can get back to honoring her memory." The lawyer pinned his gaze on Alice. "The crux of it is that Jean has left the Beachcomber to you."

Alice cast a glance over her shoulder, thinking there must be someone seated behind her, but there was no one there. She looked back at the lawyer and blinked. "To me?"

Her mother frowned. "Surely, you mean the whole family."

"No," Jeffrey said. "Jean left the Beachcomber solely to Alice."

There was an awkward silence as everyone digested the news.

Finally, her mother sucked in an indignant breath. "She did that just to get under my skin."

Alice looked at her mother with a mixture of wonder and annoyance.

Freddie leaned over and whispered, "Death brings out her narcissism."

"Only death?" Jessica muttered.

Alice felt faint. Why would Aunt Jean leave the Beachcomber to her? They weren't particularly close, and Alice didn't know the first thing about the wine business. She had a career and a home in the city.

"I don't understand," she murmured.

"Is there a letter or some explanation as to why she chose Alice of all people?" her mother asked. She reached over to pat Alice's hand. "No offense, dear."

"There's no explanation, I'm afraid," the lawyer said.

Her mother shot an aggrieved look at Alice, as though she had somehow orchestrated this outcome.

"I don't see why you're so worked up about it," Finn said to his mother. "It's not like Aunt Jean would've left it to you. You hadn't spoken in years."

Her mother glowered at Finn.

"We need more wine," Jessica said.

Freddie broke into a smile. "Well, you're in the right place."

"I suppose we should ask the new owner if it's okay to open another bottle," Finn said.

Nausea rolled over Alice. Did her brother have to be such a jerk? She didn't choose this.

"That's enough, Finn," her dad said.

"Does this mean we own a winery now?" Keegan asked.

Alice was still reeling from the news. "I guess we do for the moment. I suppose I can sell it. I don't know. I'll have to think it over."

Her father's eyes rounded. "You can't sell this place. It's been in our family for generations."

"The Beachcomber isn't a hundred years old, Dad," Freddie said.

"I'm talking about the land," he replied. "That's Hughes territory. We have a history here and I'd like us to have a future as well. If you sell this place, you'll sell a major part of our legacy."

"It isn't your decision, dear," Penny said, placing a hand on his wrist. "What happens to the Beachcomber now is entirely up to Alice."

The statement brought tears of frustration to Alice's eyes and she balled her hands into fists. "I...I don't know what to say."

Jeffrey gave her a sympathetic smile. "You're not required to say or do anything."

Finn continued to gaze at her in disbelief. "I can't believe she left you the whole shebang. Why not divide it equally between us?"

"I guess she figured you already had a business of your own," Alice said. It was a feeble excuse, but it was the only one she had.

"I didn't realize you were still in contact with Aunt Jean," her mother said, and Alice heard the accusatory tone. Alice was supposed to be loyal to her mother, which meant no fraternizing with the enemy.

"I wasn't." Alice felt flustered. "I haven't been." Other than birthday and Christmas cards, but she wasn't about to cop to that much. She felt that any admission of contact was too incendiary under the circumstances.

"It's probably because Alice is a lawyer with a good head on her shoulders and Aunt Jean knew the Beachcomber would be safe in her hands," Chelsea said.

"Sure, if the Beachcomber needs a new trademark, Alice is the perfect person to handle it. What about the rest of the business?" Finn stood, his face now covered in red splotches.

Alice recognized her brother's look. She'd seen it many times over the years, from striking out in a baseball game to missing out on the venue he wanted for his wedding. Finn hated to lose and, in his mind, he'd somehow lost the Beachcomber to his older sister.

"I need air," Alice said.

She pushed her chair back with such force, she nearly knocked it over in the process. She hurried from the table before anyone could stop her. Once outside, she was grateful that the venue was closed to the public for the memorial service. The last thing she wanted was for anyone to see her in a distressed state. She was embarrassed enough to have had an outburst in front of her kids. Ever since Greg's death, she made a point of keeping it together.

Alice hurried toward the vineyard. She could disappear in there. Buy herself time to process the news. Before she could duck behind a row of vines, a figure emerged. He was tall, probably six-foot-three, with dark blonde hair and eyes so deeply brown, they seemed to absorb all the light around him. Upon closer scrutiny, Alice recalled that he'd introduced himself earlier, but his identity was a blur.

He immediately noticed her tears. "Everything okay?" He closed his eyes in apparent mortification. "What am I saying? You're here for Jean's memorial service. Of course you're not."

Alice fished a tissue from her pocket and wiped her cheeks dry. "Sorry, just some unexpected news that threw me for a loop."

"Unwelcome news at a memorial service is a double whammy."

"I'll be fine," she said. "Thanks for asking, though."

He seemed reluctant to leave her. "I'll be inside if you or your family need anything. Don't hesitate to ask."

Alice nodded and continued forward, eager to end the conversation. She didn't want to talk to anyone right now. She wanted to listen to the sounds of nature and be alone with her thoughts.

CHAPTER SIX

CHELSEA STOOD in front of the sculpture known as Reclining Figure at LongHouse Reserve in East Hampton. No matter how many times she saw the artwork, it still reminded her of a hippo in ecstasy. Today she found herself feeling envious of the hippo. It had been months since she'd experienced any ecstasy of her own and it seemed wrong that a metal animal should be enjoying herself more than Chelsea.

"Mom, come on!"

Daniel had already moved on, disinterested in anything abstract. He preferred the sculpture of the giant chess set because it was an object he recognized. He was like his father that way. Chelsea could never persuade Brendan to join them anyplace remotely artistic. He preferred Michael Bay movies and football.

"I want to see the turtles," Daniel said. He was one shade of emotion short of stomping his foot and demanding an Oompa-Loompa.

"I'll take him if you want to stay here." Daphne swooped in to her rescue. Sweet, responsible Daphne. Only fourteen, she possessed the maturity of someone much older and wiser. Chelsea was often mystified by her oldest child. Neither Chelsea nor Brendan could claim to have been as together at thirty as Daphne seemed to be at fourteen.

"That's okay, I'm ready to walk." Chelsea didn't want to look at the sculpture anymore. Turtles were more her style at the moment anyway.

They walked to Peter's Pond and Chelsea watched as Ava opened an app on her phone and began to draw one of the water lilies on the screen with her finger. She didn't even use a stylus, and Chelsea knew the likeness would be incredible. Ava was only twelve, yet she was already a gifted artist. Over the years, every teacher at school felt compelled to tell Chelsea what a talented child Ava was and did Chelsea plan to enroll her in art classes? Chelsea usually smiled and told them yes, knowing it was a lie. She'd tried repeatedly to interest Ava in art classes, but the child refused to entertain the idea. Even at her age, she didn't want to be told what to draw or how to draw it, and Chelsea saw no reason to squelch her daughter's confidence. There would be plenty of other people in Ava's life to chip away at her armor. Her mother didn't need to be one of them. Chelsea had endured a lack of support from her mother and she had no desire to inflict the same upon her children.

"Are you mad at Aunt Alice?" Daphne asked.

Chelsea frowned. "Of course not. Why would you ask that?"

"At the Beachcomber," Daphne said, "when the lawyer told us that Alice was inheriting the winery, people seemed annoyed. I thought you might be, too."

Chelsea hugged herself to stave off the chill in the air. "I don't think I've ever been angry at Aunt Alice. She's my best friend." And she'd been through hell. If anyone deserved something as unexpected and wonderful as the winery, it was her big sister.

Daphne snorted. "You can still be mad. Sophie's my best friend and I still get mad at her sometimes."

"I think it's great," Chelsea said truthfully. "I'm just not sure whether Alice agrees." She hadn't spoken to her sister since the memorial service. She was giving Alice time to process before she checked on her. Alice wasn't someone who dove headfirst into situations and Chelsea had no doubt this unexpected development had rattled her to the core.

"Look! A mom and two babies." Daniel pointed to three turtles at the water's edge. Sensing danger from an enthusiastic boy, the mother turtle slipped beneath the surface and the two smaller turtles followed suit.

"They must be hungry," Chelsea said.

Daniel's expression crumpled. He wanted to see more of the turtles.

Daphne shuffled to his side. "Here. I managed to get a picture." She showed him her phone and his disappointment quickly faded.

Chelsea silently thanked the universe for her oldest child. Never would she have anticipated that the red-faced, screaming baby in the Bugaboo stroller would turn into this calm, clear-headed young woman. Chelsea and Brendan were often at their wit's end with their first baby. They'd been woefully unprepared for parenthood and, although her mother was nearby, Ruthie wasn't the kind of mother who offered help or advice without a sting in the tail.

Ava rubbed her finger hard across the screen and made a disgruntled sound.

"What's wrong?" Chelsea asked.

"I have to start over. It wasn't right."

Chelsea had glimpsed the image of the water lilies on Ava's screen before she deleted it and was inclined to disagree, but she knew better than to argue with the artist, especially when she was the same way with her writing.

Chelsea shoved the thought aside. She didn't want to think about her writing. If she didn't finish her current project on schedule, she was going to be fired. It would be her third missed deadline in a row, and her editor had told her in no uncertain terms that his patience was reaching an end. Chelsea couldn't help herself, though. If the words weren't right, they weren't right, and she refused to turn something in that wasn't her best work.

"A frog!" Daniel rushed closer to the pond for a better view. He twisted to look at his sister. "Can you draw him, Ava?"

"I can, but I don't want to."

Daphne heaved a sigh. "It's one frog."

"Take a picture of it and let him draw the frog when we get home," Ava said.

Chelsea thought it was a good compromise, plus it would give Daniel something to focus on when they arrived home, which would free Chelsea to make dinner without a chatty shadow. Sometimes she let Daniel act as her assistant chef, but she wasn't in the mood today. Something was bugging her and she wasn't entirely sure what.

You're in a mood, Brendan would say. Not grumpy, per se. Just a mood. According to Alice, perimenopause was to blame.

"We should probably go soon," Chelsea said. "I need time to make dinner."

"We could get pizza," Daniel said hopefully.

Chelsea ruffled his hair. It was the same strawberry blonde as his father's and Chelsea thought there wasn't a more beautiful hair color in the world. "Another time," she said.

. . .

The Carter 'beach house' was located in East Hampton, south of the highway in a position Isabel identified as 'beachfront adjacent.' Although it didn't boast a water view, there was a short, private path to the beach. The white house with black trim boasted seven bedrooms, a two-car garage, a heated gunite pool, and, of course, a pool house.

Isabel parked in front of the white porte-cochere, designed to match the house. She didn't see another car and began to worry that she'd gotten the date or time wrong. It was possible there was a car in the garage, but in Isabel's experience, nobody used their garage for its intended purpose. If there was an actual car in the garage, it was likely an expensive antique that only existed to be admired rather than driven.

Isabel rang the bell and waited. No answer. She started to rummage through her purse for her phone to confirm the details. She found Brianna's text and frowned. No, she was definitely here at the right time. She was about to text Brianna and ask for the brother's phone number when it occurred to her to check the pool house first. Maybe he was waiting for her there rather than at the main house. It made sense, given the pool house was the reason she was here.

Isabel skirted the outside of the house and made her way to the backyard. She stopped in her tracks when she rounded the corner and got a glimpse of the outdoor space. The breathtaking backyard was a true oasis. Isabel could easily picture herself living out here full-time. Pull out a few heat lamps in the winter and she'd be perfectly content. The pool was much larger than others she'd enjoyed in the Hamptons. It was no wonder the pool house was spacious enough to warrant a redesign.

"Nice, right?"

Isabel whirled around to see a dark-haired man in a Columbia T-shirt and basketball shorts. Isabel's immediate thought was that he was undeniably handsome and she immediately squelched it. Rocky or not, she and Jackson were still involved. She had no business letting her head be turned by an attractive stranger.

"It's stunning," Isabel said, recovering her voice. "I expected it to be grand, but this is something else."

He offered his hand. "I'm Mason Briggs. Sorry, I didn't hear you arrive. I was in the gym."

As she shook his hand, Isabel averted her gaze. The moment felt too intimate, which was, of course, ridiculous. She shook hands with people every day, and always made eye contact.

"No problem," she said. "I didn't see a car, so I started to worry I'd gotten the time wrong."

"Not at all. It's me. I'm terrible at keeping track of time. Brianna is constantly trying to break me of the habit."

"Ah, she must be your older sister then."

He chuckled. "Sounds like you know a thing or two about older siblings."

She clasped her hands in front of her. "I do. I have three older ones and one younger one."

Mason whistled. "Busy parents."

Isabel broke into a smile. "Only my father. My older three have a different mom."

The corner of his mouth turned up. "I guess yours is Smurfette."

It took Isabel a second to get the joke. Her hair had been blue for two months now, so she was used to it. "Big Smurfs fan, huh?"

"I may have watched a show or two in my youth. What's your natural color?"

"I'm a blonde, like my mom."

"Thought so." He shifted his attention to the pool house. "Ready to check it out? Or would you rather I shower first?" He held out his arms. "I promise not to be insulted if you don't want to be in close proximity to my sweaty body."

Warmth radiated through her own body at the prospect. "I can handle it," she said. "Two brothers, remember?"

Together, they crossed the lawn to the pool house and Mason opened the door, motioning for her to enter first.

"Brianna mentioned you're living at the house temporarily," Isabel said. She told herself she was merely making conversation rather than fishing for information.

"My place is being renovated. My wife got the house in the divorce, so I bought a new one and, naturally, decided to tear it down to the studs." He laughed. "The kind of thing I do that drove my wife crazy, hence the divorce."

"Any kids?" The question popped out of Isabel's mouth before she could stop it. She wasn't one to ask personal questions of strangers. She considered it rude, as did her mother. It was one of the reasons they had a hard time tolerating Ruthie. Ruthie would ask you the details of your colonoscopy if she knew you'd had one. How many polyps and where were they located? Benign? How many years until the next screening? Isabel had heard her ask these very questions of a neighbor years ago and never forgot the feeling of second-hand mortification.

"We have a son, Asher. He's seven."

"Sweet."

"He is. Loves cuddles and I'm wondering how long that phase lasts because it's pretty awesome."

"Depends on the child, I think. Finn wasn't much for cuddles, but Freddie would hug you until you lost all sensation in your torso."

Mason chuckled. "Sounds like an ex-girlfriend of mine."

"Is your son local?"

"Sag Harbor. I made sure to buy a house in the same

town, so it's easier for him to come and go, especially as he gets older."

"My sister and her family live in Sag Harbor. Chelsea and Brendan Somers. They love it there."

"Same." A grin split his face. "I'm sure my ex would've preferred I move a few miles further to get me out of her hair, but I wanted to be close by and not miss anything. We might not be together anymore, but we're going to do our duty as parents and annoy him at every school function."

Isabel laughed, as he escorted her from room to room. "My parents came to everything, and it was half mortifying and half wonderful." She surprised herself by adding, "They're still together and disgustingly happy. In fact, I think they've set the bar too high." Isabel bit down on her lip to prevent herself from saying more. She rarely divulged personal information, certainly not without being prompted. What was it about Mason Briggs that made her want to tell him unnecessary details of her life? Whatever next—her deepest, darkest secrets? She hadn't even shared those with Jackson.

"Sounds like they ought to be on display in a museum," Mason teased.

Isabel felt the heat rise to her cheeks. "Anyway, I'm sure your ex-wife is glad to have you close by for Asher's sake."

"I like your rosy outlook—and your cheeks."

Her stomach tightened and she found herself craving more signs of his approval. She wanted confirmation that he liked what he saw. The more she desired it, the more she felt like a terrible person. What would Jackson say if he knew what was running through her mind? All the swanky events she attended and she never once looked at another man since she'd started dating Jackson, no matter how fit or funny. The male species had ceased to interest her in a romantic sense.

Until now.

"What do you think?" Mason asked, cutting into her thoughts. "Are you interested?"

It took a moment for Isabel to register that he meant the pool house. "Oh, um. I'll have to think about it."

His brow lifted. "Really? I mean, I'm no designer, but I would think this would be a pretty good project."

"It isn't that. I live and work in Manhattan. If I take this on, it would mean spending time here."

His mouth quirked. "Would that be so bad?"

Yes, Isabel thought, her inside quivering. It would be very, very bad, indeed.

"I promised Brianna I would consider it, so I will."

"Well, I hope you decide to stick around. It would be nice to have company out here this time of year."

"Oh, it won't be long now before the summer people start pouring in." Isabel remembered those days well. Lazy mornings, afternoons at the beach, and evenings jam-packed with social events. She was fortunate not to suffer from FOMO, even in her teens. If she didn't feel like peopling, she simply stayed home and didn't give it another thought. She didn't mind the world spinning without her. She knew she'd jump back on the ride when she was in the mood.

Looking at Mason now, Isabel realized that she was very much in the mood.

CHAPTER SEVEN

"THE NEW OWNER IS HERE," Henri said.

Ryan gave the winemaker a crisp nod. He'd been anticipating this moment and couldn't decide how he felt about it. Jean was a terrible loss, and her name was synonymous with the Beachcomber. He'd been fond of the old woman, despite their disagreements on how to run the winery. It frustrated him that he'd been hired for a particular set of skills but was then consistently prevented from using them.

Tawny smoothed a wayward strand of hair. "Remember. I'm up first."

Henri rolled his eyes. "We know. You've told us enough times."

Ryan cast a wary glance at the winemaker. "You're not leaving, too, are you?"

The Frenchman shook his head. "No, I like it here."

Ryan thought as much but wanted confirmation. Knowing the events manager was quitting put him in an awkward position. He'd been interviewing for jobs before Jean's death and now he wasn't sure what to do if an offer came through. He felt conflicted about leaving a new owner in the lurch. She couldn't afford to lose experienced members of staff.

"Hello?" a hesitant voice called.

A brunette appeared in the doorway and Ryan balked. He recognized the crying woman from the vineyard during the memorial service. Thankfully, there were no tears now, only an apprehensive expression.

"You're Alice?" he asked.

"Yes," she said. "Alice Hughes. Jean was my father's aunt."

Ryan was the first to step forward. "Ryan McElroy. We met in the vineyard." He shook her hand and was surprised by a firm grip that seemed in direct contrast to her demeanor.

"Yes, I remember," she said.

"Henri Alicante," the winemaker said.

"Baz is in the cellar, but he'll be up shortly," Ryan said.

"He's the sommelier," Alice said, and Ryan nodded.

"I'm Tawny Stapleton, the events manager. Might I have a word before you get too busy?"

Ryan flinched. He thought Tawny would at least let the woman catch her breath before breaking the bad news. Tawny wasn't the kindest woman, though. He knew that even when he'd slept with her after a New Year's Eve party two years ago. He'd been too drunk to care about whether she was kind, only that she was willing.

Alice looked like a deer caught in the headlights. "You want a word with me?" She swiveled from left to right. "Is there an office I can use?"

"Use mine," Ryan offered. "It was Jean's to start with, but she gave it up when she stopped coming in every day."

Tawny waltzed toward the doorway. "I can show you where it is."

Henri busied himself with his usual tasks while Ryan paced the floor. He disliked the tension in the air. Despite the inconvenience, it was best that Tawny left. She wouldn't have been his choice for events manager anyway, but she'd been hired two years before him.

Alice returned to the kitchen a few minutes later, visibly rattled. "I don't suppose it's the worst news in the world. It's only March, right? No big events until summer, I assume."

Henri and Ryan exchanged uneasy glances.

"There's a rather important charity event on April thirtieth," Henri said.

"Charity event," she repeated, sounding as dazed as she looked.

"I can talk to a few recruiters, see who's out there," Ryan said, "but it won't happen fast enough to help us now."

"What does that mean?" she asked.

"It means we'll have to handle it between us," Ryan said.

Henri held up his hands. "Not me. I make wine, not events."

"I didn't mean you," Ryan said. He tried to disguise his annoyance. Henri could at least pretend to be a team player.

"So this charity event is the only thing to worry about?" Alice asked.

"The first wedding is in May," another voice chimed in. "Just around the corner."

Ryan turned toward the doorway. "Alice, this is Duke Thompson, our head vineyard manager."

Duke wiped a dirty hand on his jeans before offering it to Alice. "Sorry, I've been working outside this morning."

"Don't apologize. I should've called first. Honestly, I've been so taken aback by the whole thing, I can barely function. I almost washed my face with toothpaste last night."

Ryan smiled. There was something about her that he found endearing.

"Jean liked to pretend to forget information," Duke said,

"but I figured out pretty quickly that it was her way of testing me."

"She was exceedingly clever," Henri said, smiling.

"I'm sorry we didn't include you in the service," Alice said.

Ryan waved his hands. "No, no. That was all Jean. She arranged her own service for family and a separate one for us."

"Ours was Sunday," Henri added.

Duke barked a laugh. "She knew ours couldn't be the night before yours or we wouldn't be able to host it."

"As I said," Henri interjected, "exceedingly clever."

"You mentioned the sommelier is in the cellar. Who else is missing?" Alice asked.

"Rosalie Santos is our chef," Henri said. "She will be in later."

Alice cast a sidelong glance at Ryan. "She's not planning to jump ship?"

"Not that I know of," Ryan said. "Don't worry. I'm the general manager. Help is part of the job description."

She nodded, appearing to arrive at a decision. "Okay. I'll make arrangements to stay through the charity event. After that, I don't know. It's probably best to sell."

Ryan said nothing. The staff had discussed the possibility on Sunday, and what that might mean for them. There was a chance they could be taken over by a larger company, which had its pros and cons.

"The right buyer can take years to find," Henri warned. "Perhaps not best to pin your hopes on that option."

"I see. Thank you." Her voice was almost inaudible.

"Why don't I give you a tour?" Ryan asked. "That will help you get acclimated."

"Yes, that's a good idea," she said. "It's been years since I've spent any time here and most of that involved games in the vineyard."

"You've never had to look at this place through an owner's eyes," Ryan said. "It'll be a different experience for you now."

Alice didn't look thrilled at the prospect of a different experience.

"I am going to the cellar now," Henri said. "If you start there, I can answer any questions you have."

Alice's head wouldn't stop spinning as she followed Ryan and Henri to the cellar. Although her mother had been visibly annoyed about the contents of the will, Alice knew she'd rejoice when Alice announced she would stay in the Hamptons through the end of the month. Her mother had practically done a somersault when Alice changed her plans after the memorial service and decided to spend spring break in the Hamptons. The kids were equally excited. Only Alice was unhappy with the sudden change of plans. Quick decisions made her deeply uncomfortable, especially decisions that meant she was stuck in her mother's house in the Hamptons.

Baz was already in the cellar, choosing next month's wines for their wine club members. The sommelier was dressed in suspenders and a bowtie and his hipster beard appeared to have been trimmed since Saturday. He welcomed her with a smile and a handshake and went straight back to work.

Despite the winemaker's enthusiasm, Alice only half listened as Henri identified the different barrels in the cellar and offered details on storage. She was too worried about her firm's reaction when she requested a leave of absence. Maybe she wouldn't ask. She could request to work remotely. After all, Aunt Jean hadn't been working at the Beachcomber every day at her age. Alice could be an absentee boss until she decided on next steps—except this charity event needed her attention and Alice didn't know whether it would be feasible to divide her time between the two. It also seemed important to understand the business to the best of her ability before she made any big decisions. She wouldn't be comfortable relying solely on other people's opinions without due diligence of her own.

There were also the children to consider. She couldn't pull them out of school. Thankfully, spring break bought her a little time but not the whole month.

"Any questions so far?" Henri asked.

"Not yet," she said. "I'm sure I'll have some eventually, though."

She and Ryan left the cellar and walked through the vineyard, where Ryan spouted off types of grapes and more facts than Alice could memorize. It had been many years since law school and she'd been practicing in her current field for so long that she worked on autopilot most of the time.

Ryan seemed to read her mind. "You don't have to learn it all in one day," he assured her. "This is an overview."

"You seem to know everything there is to know about this place," she said. "How long have you worked here?"

"Four—almost five years, but I worked at similar places in New Zealand and California before this."

"Aunt Jean lured you to the Hamptons from there?" Alice couldn't imagine trading either of those places for Southampton.

"It's beautiful here," Ryan said, "especially the North Fork. I head out there whenever I get free time."

Roughly parallel to the Hamptons, the North Fork was another Long Island peninsula. Alice had childhood memories of horseback riding on the North Fork, but she wasn't interested in reminiscing right now.

"Jeffrey mentioned reviewing the books with the accountant," Alice said. "I assume you can help me arrange that."

"Of course. Mike Wallace. I'm happy to join you in any meetings, too. Be an extra set of eyes and ears."

Alice was thrilled by that idea. Yes, someone knowledgeable by her side would take the edge off. She was competent and intelligent—she knew that about herself—but she also felt entirely out of her depth at the Beachcomber.

"Thank you. I'd appreciate that."

"Great. I'll schedule an appointment with Mike. Any days better for you?"

Alice thought of the kids' school schedule next week and laughed. "They're all bad."

Ryan didn't seem put off. "I'll see what I can do."

"My kids start back at school in the city on Monday and, if I'm staying here, I need to figure out childcare. I'm a widow, so there isn't anyone else at home with them." She wasn't sure why she felt the need to explain, probably because she didn't want Ryan to think she was being a pain for the sake of it, like people who sent food back to the restaurant kitchen just because they could.

"I'm sorry to hear that." He paused. "Your husband...He was the one with pancreatic cancer?"

Alice bit her lip. "Yes. Three years ago."

"Right. Jean talked about you both." His expression shifted and Alice got the sense he was remembering more. "Now I get it."

"Get what?"

"Why you're the new owner. I hadn't put it together before."

Alice frowned. "She told you why she chose me?"

"Not in so many words, but she said you were the one most able to handle challenges," he said.

Alice offered a rueful smile. "I wish her decision hadn't upset other people in my family."

"I don't think that was her intention."

"No, of course not." Aunt Jean wasn't like that. Her mother, on the other hand, was a different story.

He stopped walking and looked at her. "Jean and I worked closely together. She was very much a part of the business, right up until the end. She was hardworking, smart, and had a good sense of humor, and I was very fond of her."

Her smile became less pained. "Thank you for telling me that. I regret not making more of an effort with her in recent years. It was hard with the animosity. My mother..." She trailed off. "It doesn't matter. We're here to talk about the Beachcomber, not the Beachcomber's messy family."

Ryan flicked a vine with his fingers. "Winemaking is messy, too. Seems to me you're a perfect match."

CHAPTER EIGHT

FREDDIE GAZED at the ceiling in the guest room of his parents' house, observing the blades of the fan as they whirled overhead. He didn't much care about circulating the air. He just liked watching the movement. It helped focus his mind and kept his thoughts from jumping around too much. Right now, he was trying to focus on the conversation he was about to have with his folks. They would be none too pleased when they heard that Freddie was unemployed. Again.

A creaky step warned him that someone was awake and headed downstairs. His mother, he guessed. She had more energy than anyone he knew. Certainly more than his dad.

Freddie kicked off the covers and prepared to rise. If his mother was alone, then he might break the news to her first and, together, they could decide how to handle his father. Hunton Hughes wasn't as laidback as his wife and Freddie knew there was a chance his father might boot him from the house in anger, not that Freddie minded going back to the city. He only attended the memorial service out of respect for his dad and to catch up with Chelsea and Finn, whom he didn't see very often. He hadn't known Aunt Jean well enough to have feelings about her death one way or the other. The only point in the old woman's favor was that she'd been sensible enough to break off contact with Ruthie years ago. Plus, she owned a wine business with a hot sommelier. Another point in her favor.

Freddie peered into the hallway before daring to venture downstairs. He heard movement in the kitchen, which meant the active party was definitely his mother. His dad was more likely to sit at the table and read until someone appeared to feed and water him.

His mom broke into a bright smile at the sight of him. "Good morning, sweetheart."

"Hi, Mom." He inhaled the rich aroma of brewing coffee and sank onto a stool at the counter.

"How'd you sleep?" His mother was in a perpetual state of motion. She reminded Freddie of that movie with Keanu Reeves and Sandra Bullock, where the bus couldn't slow below 50 miles per hour, or it would explode. Sometimes he worried he'd find pieces of his mom scattered in all directions and would know that it was because she'd encountered an obstacle too formidable to pass.

"Fine." In truth, he hated the mattress in the guest room— it was too firm, but he wasn't here frequently enough to complain. "Not to rush perfection, but is the coffee ready yet?"

"Almost." She opened the refrigerator and contemplated the options. "Eggs? Or would you rather I make pancakes?" She glanced over her shoulder, smiling at him. "I can add chocolate chips and whipped cream."

Freddie ducked his head. "Mom, I'm thirty-three, not three."

"So what? Who says you're not allowed to like special

pancakes after adolescence?" She reached across the counter to ruffle his hair.

Freddie decided now might be a good time to share his misery. The house was still quiet and his mom was in a cheerful mood.

"I'd like scrambled eggs, please," he said. He'd wait until she became preoccupied with cracking eggs, and then she could picture the egg as his skull. Everyone needed an outlet for their frustrations.

"I'll get started. Your father should be down soon. He was stirring when I got up." She danced her way over to the cabinet and retrieved two mugs.

Freddie bit back a smile. His mom was the only person he knew who danced around a room without music.

"Do you want the one with the dog?" She held up the mug for his inspection. "That's your favorite, isn't it?"

"I don't know that I have a favorite, but it's fine." The mug featured the image of a Yorkshire terrier, which had amused him as a child because they'd never had a dog.

His mother poured two cups of coffee and slid the dog mug over to Freddie. She took a single sip of hers before returning to the refrigerator for the eggs.

"There's something I want to tell you," Freddie said. His stomach was tangled in knots. It didn't matter how many times he'd had a conversation like this one, he was still a mess.

"Are you back together with Sam?"

"No, no. That was…No."

"Good, I wasn't a fan."

"You didn't even meet him."

"I know. I'm basing this on things you and Isabel told me."

Freddie would have to question his sister on exactly what information she'd shared with their mother.

"It's about work." Freddie rubbed the back of his neck.

He'd have a stress zit on his face by tomorrow, he just knew it.

"Go on." His mother continued with her breakfast prep, but he could tell she was listening. It was one of her strengths, letting you know that you're being heard even when she's busy with another task.

Freddie inhaled deeply before setting the truth free. "I got fired."

His mother set a pan on the stovetop and turned to face him. "This is the job Brendan arranged for you?" She didn't sound angry, just curious.

He nodded. "It wasn't a performance issue. They were happy with my work."

She licked her lips. "But?"

"I failed a random drug test."

His mother pursed her lips and squeezed her eyes shut. It was the most emotion she'd show over his failure, he knew that much.

"Please tell me it was pot."

"It was pot."

She turned back to the eggs and began cracking them open into a bowl with admirable restraint. Maybe not picturing his skull then.

"Does Brendan know?" she asked.

"Not yet, I don't think. He didn't mention it at the memorial service."

She moved the bowl of eggs to the counter in front of Freddie and whisked them. "What's your plan, Frederick Hunton Hughes?"

Egads, the full name. Freddie swallowed a mouthful of coffee and let the rich flavor coat his tongue. "Still thinking."

"Thinking doesn't pay the bills." She returned to the stovetop and dumped the contents of the bowl into the preheated pan. Freddie heard the satisfying hiss of heat as the eggs made contact.

"I'll figure something out." He always landed on his feet. His friends called him Don Gato because they likened him to a cat.

"Why don't you talk to Finn? I bet he'd take you on. You could stay in the Hamptons and get your realtor's license."

Freddie snorted. "Mom, seriously. We'd kill each other and you know it. We already have one young widow in the family. Do we really need another? What is it Ruthie likes to say—*people will talk?*"

His mother's shoulders rounded and Freddie could tell she was stifling a laugh. Obviously, Greg's death wasn't funny, but Freddie refused to let any topic be too precious. He'd been overly fond of his burly brother-in-law—the Oaf as he affectionately called him—and joined in the family's grief.

"Can we not tell your father about this, at least for now?"

Freddie was surprised by the request. His parents didn't keep secrets from each other; it had been a rule throughout his childhood. When Freddie confided in his mom that he got a D in geometry, he knew it was only a matter of time before she told his dad. When Freddie got his first speeding ticket, he knew his mom would inevitably tell his dad. Rules are rules.

"Is something wrong?" he asked.

His mother shifted the eggs around in the pan. "His doctor wants him to take it easy, so I don't want to give him news that will stress him out."

"Then maybe he shouldn't have been allowed to wrestle that cork at the Beachcomber."

They both started laughing.

"Poor Ruthie," his mother said. "And you know I don't say that often."

"Or ever." He paused. "Is it his heart?" Hunton Hughes was a large man, although not particularly overweight. Penny had insisted on a healthy diet for the whole family, no exceptions.

"Nothing serious," she said. "I'd just rather hold off for now."

"Then you'd better tell Chelsea and Brendan. They're likely to say something once they find out."

She turned to look at him and, for the first time, Freddie noticed the fine lines around her eyes and mouth. His mother was younger than his father and had always struck Freddie as eternally youthful, but he couldn't deny that age finally seemed to be catching up to her.

"Let's keep it our little secret, okay?"

Freddie nodded and drank the remainder of his coffee. Although he was pleased to avoid his father's disappointed glare, he couldn't help but feel uneasy about the reason.

"Why don't you stay longer if there's no rush to get back? We can tell everyone you took vacation days."

Freddie brought his empty mug to the pot for a refill. "Can't. I have a date on Thursday night."

"Who makes a date for a Thursday night?" she asked. "What's wrong with a Friday or Saturday?"

Freddie smiled. "That's too much of a commitment. A Thursday night is more relaxed."

His mother slid the eggs onto a serving platter. "I'm starting to believe you're one of those commitment phobes."

Despite his poor record, Freddie didn't think so. "Thursday was his suggestion," he said, as though that answered the question.

"Is it serious?"

He returned to his place on the stool. "I haven't even been out with him yet, so no." He'd met Paul at a brunch with friends and they'd hit it off. Freddie wasn't sure Paul was his type, but he tried never to limit his options. If a social invitation was extended, Freddie was there with bells on.

"Why not reschedule? I'm sure he'll understand."

"Reschedule what?" His father entered the kitchen, seeming to fill all the space around him. He wore his trademark plaid flannel pajama set. Freddie was pretty sure his father would request to be buried in similar attire, slippers and newspaper included.

"Freddie has a date, but I'm trying to convince him to cancel and stay longer."

"If you can get the time off work, why not?" his father said. "You can buy just about anything with money except time."

Freddie shot a quizzical glance at his mother. It wasn't like his father to sound so philosophical. Maybe his mother was downplaying the heart condition. If she was willing to keep a secret about Freddie from her husband, then maybe she was willing to do the reverse.

"I'll see what I can do," Freddie said. If his dad was dealing with a health issue, then Freddie wanted to know. And the best way to suss it out was to hang around. The truth about Freddie's job was bound to come out eventually anyway. Brendan could easily find out from his friend, Kurt, who'd put in a good word for Freddie.

His father took his place at the table, awaiting service. "Excellent. I was in the mood for eggs."

His mom carried over a plate and set it in front of him. "I must've sensed it." She kissed the side of his head. "Hot water with lemon?"

His eyes turned downcast. "If you insist."

His mother winked at Freddie as she sailed across the kitchen to fill the kettle. Nothing ever seemed to be a burden for her. Freddie liked that about his mother. She seemed to revel in the act of Taking Care of Her Family. Freddie knew from listening to his half siblings that Ruthie was more of the martyr type. It baffled him that his father would have ever married a woman like Ruthie in the first place. He and Penny seemed so right for each other. Freddie hoped that if he ever married, he'd get it right the first time.

CHAPTER NINE

LIVING IN THE CITY, brunch at Pierre's in Bridgehampton was one activity Isabel missed, so she was thrilled when her sister suggested meeting there. She loved the charming outdoor seating in the heart of town, although she was perfectly content to sit inside, too.

She spotted her sister alone at a table by the window. Her dark head was bent over a notebook and she was scribbling furiously, as though trying to get the thoughts on paper before they dissipated.

"I guess you miss this place, too," Isabel said.

Alice looked up and smiled. "If I could take it with me to the city, I would." She stood and greeted Isabel with a kiss on the cheek. "I'm glad you decided to stay longer, too."

Isabel slid into the chair across from her. "I promised a client I would consider taking on a project in East Hampton, so I went to have a look and decided to start on it right away." She'd meditated on it afterward and her gut told her to stick around.

"Someone mentioned a beach house?"

"A pool house that they use as a guest house," she clarified. "Brianna's one of my best clients. I could hardly say no." At least, that was what she kept telling herself to justify the decision. It also helped that Isabel had earmarked the next few weeks to work on Brianna's city apartment. Now that the room was no longer in need of chintz, Isabel's schedule was wide open.

"What will Jackson do without you?" Alice teased.

Isabel kept her smile firmly in place. She didn't want to ruin their brunch with negativity. "He's a grownup. He'll figure out where the new rolls of toilet paper are stored."

"At least we got to see him at the memorial service," Alice said. "I wish we saw the two of you more often in the city, though."

"You're as bad as we are when it comes to work," Isabel said. Her sister didn't argue.

"Are you going to stay with Dad and Penny?" Alice asked.

"No, in my client's guest house," Isabel said.

Alice gave her a knowing smile. "The fully immersive experience."

The server brought two peach Bellinis that Alice had ordered for them, as well as two plates of French toast.

"You sneaky devil," Isabel said, delighted that Alice knew exactly what to order. Of course she did. Alice had always been the ideal older sister.

"I had to get our order in before ten-thirty or we'd have to order from the other menu," Alice explained. She moved aside her notebook to make room for the plate.

Isabel peered across the table for a better view. "What are you working on?"

Her sister heaved a weary sigh. "A pros and cons list about the Beachcomber."

Isabel laughed. "Some things never change." She tried to steal the notebook away, but Alice was too quick for her. She pinned the notebook to the table, holding it firmly in place.

"Not this time, little sister," Alice said. "I need this list to process my thoughts."

"Why not try to feel your way through an issue for once?" Isabel asked.

Alice cut her a sideways glance. "I don't even know what that means in practical terms."

Isabel blew a raspberry. "Because it isn't practical. Just think about the Beachcomber and ask yourself whether it feels right to keep it."

Alice appeared unconvinced. "I think a list makes more sense."

"Did you make a list when Greg asked you to marry him?"

Alice flinched and Isabel felt slightly guilty for invoking his name. Her older sister clearly had enough on her mind without throwing Greg into the mental maelstrom.

"As it happens, I did." Alice flashed a triumphant smile. "There were seven reasons in the pros column and four in the cons column, so I married him."

Isabel couldn't imagine making a list in order to make a decision of the heart. She liked Jackson and thought he was cute, so when he asked her out, she said yes. There'd been no debate, no weighing of reasons for and against. Of course, maybe if Isabel had been one to make lists, she would've already reached a decision about other important matters before they threw her life into chaos.

"Dare I ask what the four cons were?" Isabel asked.

Alice gazed at the page, as though envisioning the answers there. "Messy. Leaves laundry on the floor and the kitchen dirty."

Isabel snorted. "Sounds like me."

"Forgets important dates. Leaves me to plan everything. Doesn't apologize."

Isabel was slightly taken aback. She'd expected the

reasons to be more trivial than those, like prefers dogs to cats.

"Did any of those change after you got married?"

"We hired a weekly cleaner once we could afford it, so that eliminated the first one, for the most part."

Isabel sensed that the other three cons remained persistent problems throughout the marriage. "How about the seven pros? In hindsight, would you say they outweighed the cons?"

"I loved Greg and we have two wonderful children," Alice said, as though that answered the question. "To be honest, I haven't thought about that list in ages."

Isabel regarded her for a long moment. "You kept it, though, didn't you? I bet it's in your bedside drawer."

Alice burst into laughter. "Close. In the top drawer of my desk." She paused, her expression growing dreamy. "Greg found it not long after we were married. He had it laminated and gave it to me as a gift for Valentine's Day."

Isabel clucked her tongue. "And you said he didn't remember dates."

Her sister seemed to enjoy the memory, which made Isabel feel better about raising the subject.

"I guess if you're taking on this beach house, then there's no chance you can stay at the apartment with the kids until I decide what to do with the Beachcomber. The kids can't miss school."

Isabel's expression crumpled. "Oh, wow. I would love to, but I can't if I'm working on the Carter guest house."

"Right, of course."

"Do you need to be here? Can't you just go back to the city and make a decision from there?"

Alice toyed with her fork. "You know me. I need to research thoroughly before I reach a decision. Besides, the family will freak out if I sell it without giving it careful consideration. I need to be able to back up my reasoning."

"If it's any consolation, I won't freak out. I want you to do what's best for you."

Alice smiled. "Thanks. I appreciate that."

Isabel brought the glass to her lips. "Although I can imagine Finn's reaction if you sell."

Alice shook her head. "I'd rather not imagine it. Nightmare."

"Who knows? Maybe you'll fall in love with the Beachcomber and decide to quit your job."

Alice swallowed a mouthful of Bellini and began to cough.

Isabel laughed. "Or not."

"I told the staff I'd at least stay through this charity event they're hosting, since it's a big deal. It was Aunt Jean's pet project, so I'd like to give it my full attention and make sure it goes off without a hitch. I owe her that much."

"What about Freddie for the kids?" Isabel suggested. "His office is in midtown. He could be there when the kids leave for school and be back in time to order dinner."

Alice hesitated. "I'm not sure he's the right person for the job."

Isabel understood her sister's reluctance. Keegan would likely be parenting Freddie more than the other way around.

"Do you have another option?"

Alice seemed to mull it over. "My mom's retired now, but the thought of her in my apartment...Anyway, the kids would kill me. They adore Uncle Freddie, though."

"As they should. He's the perfect uncle. Besides, what's the worst that can happen with Freddie in charge? Junk food for a month or so won't kill them."

Alice nodded to herself. "I'll talk to him."

"What about your firm? Are you going to ask to work remotely?"

Alice wiped a napkin across her mouth. "I actually requested an emergency leave of absence."

Isabel tried to contain her shock. She knew her sister would take the Beachcomber situation seriously, but she didn't expect quite this level of commitment.

"I was surprised they agreed to it," Alice continued. "They're not great about accommodating requests, but the department lost a big client recently and we're light on matters right now. Anyway, I'm glad it worked out."

"Me, too." Isabel remembered the hard time the firm gave her sister after Greg's death. They'd made Alice personally find other lawyers in the department to take over her work-load before she could take time off to grieve with her kids. Isabel would've been out the door, but not Alice. She'd returned at the earliest opportunity and buried herself in work.

"At first, I worried about taking time away from the kids. They already function without one parent..." Her gaze dropped to the table. "I spoke to them about it, and they said they'd be fine."

Isabel leaned forward. "No maternal guilt! This is a golden opportunity for you. Your kids won't wilt. They're teenagers now. They're not even supposed to like you."

Alice arched an eyebrow. "Am I supposed to like them? Some days, I'm not so sure."

Isabel warmed to the plan. "You can be a free woman in the Hamptons. Nobody says you have to spend all your waking hours at the Beachcomber. Aunt Jean certainly didn't."

"Only because her waking hours only lasted between the hours of eleven and four."

Isabel snorted. "Still, take advantage of this. Do what you

have to do at the Beachcomber, of course, but take time for yourself."

"Kind of hard, if I stay here with my mother."

"Is Ruthie being her usual self?"

"If that's code for a pain in the ass, then yes. She's being her usual self."

"Still pushing the dating apps?" Isabel asked.

"Naturally."

Isabel chewed thoughtfully. "Would it be so bad?"

Her sister's jaw unhinged. "Hey! Whose side are you on?"

"Your mom is a pain, but she's not wrong. Not this time, anyway."

"Et tu, Brutus?" Alice shook her head. "I have my hands full under normal circumstances. Now, with the Beachcomber...Well, there's no way dating fits into my new schedule." She paused. "I just want to do the right thing."

"No," Isabel said firmly. "You want to do the thing that makes the most people happy, even if it doesn't make you happy."

"You say that like it's a bad thing."

"This is your life, Alice. You have to live it for *you*." She shoved a forkful of French toast into her mouth and relished the taste.

"It's different when you have kids," Alice said. "You have to put their needs first."

"As long as you're not using them as a shield from the rest of the world."

"Talk to me again when you have children," Alice said, not unkindly.

Isabel fell silent. Her sister didn't know...Not that it mattered. Alice was right. Isabel wasn't a mother and she could understand how that role might shift priorities.

"I keep waiting for Finn and Jessica to announce they're pregnant," Alice continued.

"Do you think they will?" Isabel asked. "I always got the impression that Jessica wanted to focus on her career."

"Maybe, but I can't see Finn forgoing the chance to have a mini-Finn running around. It's a pathway to immortality."

Isabel snorted again, and this time water almost came out her nose. "Only Finn would view parenthood as a pathway to godhood."

"At the memorial service, when Amelia asked her about having kids…" Alice's brow furrowed. "Her reaction was odd."

Isabel wondered whether Alice had picked up on her own reaction. If she had, she was too polite to admit it now. She was grateful when the server interrupted to ask if they wanted to order anything else. They declined in unison and the server dropped the check and moved on to the next table.

Alice patted her stomach. "I think I've done enough damage for one day."

"Same," Isabel said. "But it was fun. We should do it again while we're here."

"Definitely." Alice raised her glass. "Cheers to being back in the Hamptons together. Next time, let's make sure Chelsea can join us."

"She's got three kids enrolled in all manner of activities. Face it, Alice. You and I are the ladies who brunch now."

CHAPTER TEN

BIRDS SQUAWKED OVERHEAD, nearly drowning out Duke's voice as he explained the importance of the trellising system. Alice strained to listen, typing notes on her phone. *Support. Minimize disease. Sun exposure. Canopy management.* She had ample experience synthesizing unfamiliar information into something manageable. Her inner voice told her repeatedly that she could handle this. If she said it enough times, maybe she'd start to believe it.

"You should be grateful this isn't harvest season," Duke said. "Talk about throwing you into the deep end."

Alice smiled. "You can still drown in an inch of water."

His eyes danced with amusement. "That you can."

"What got you interested in vineyards?" she asked.

"A trip to France when I was in high school. My dad wanted me to join the military and become a JAG and I'd been considering it until that trip." He paused to smile at her. "I still remember my dad's reaction when I told him my plans. 'Black men don't work a job like that, son.' At the time, I was pissed off, but I understood later that he was trying to save me from disappointment."

"And here you are," Alice said. "No disappointment necessary."

His gaze shifted to the acres of vines. "I feel sorry for people who never find their passion, don't you?"

Alice didn't know how to respond. Duke assumed she was like him, but she could hardly describe intellectual property law as her passion. It was a solid career choice, nothing more, and that was fine with her.

"If everyone followed their passion, who would sweep the floors at night?" she asked.

Duke laughed lightly. "Sounds like an adult got to you before you had a chance to dream."

"I'm satisfied with my choices," Alice said.

Duke nodded approvingly. "Then I guess that's all that matters."

The sound of quick footsteps diverted her attention to the pathway. Ryan jogged toward them in a dark blue suit.

"Sorry, I'm late. The lights finally got delivered," he said.

"We're going to need as many hands as we've got to get those lights set up out here," Duke said. He cut a quick glance at Alice. "We're going to put up over fifteen thousand LED lights for the Light Up Your Life charity event."

"Wow. Do you need to hire temporary help for that?" Alice asked. She still remembered how long it took her father to put up the Christmas lights for one modest house. She couldn't imagine dealing with over fifteen thousand.

Ryan looked at Duke. "We've got enough people to handle it." It was more of a confirmation than a question.

Duke blew out a breath. "Yeah, but we'll need to get started. I wish the lights had come in when they originally said."

Alice cocked her head. "Is there a problem I need to know about?"

Ryan clapped her on the shoulder. "It's taken care of. Lights are here now. It's my job to deal with any problems."

Alice tried to relax. She wasn't used to someone else tackling problems. She was the fixer. The guardian. But it was a nice change of pace to sit back and let another adult handle an issue.

Ryan surveyed the vineyard. "So, how's it going out here? Learning anything?"

She sucked in a breath. "I won't lie. It's a lot to digest." And a lot of land to walk. "How often did Aunt Jean come out to inspect the vineyard?"

"One of us would drive her around in a golf cart," Duke said. "She loved being out here as much as possible. She said it kept her young."

Alice could see why. With sunlight pouring over the vines, this place was absolutely stunning. "I don't remember ever thinking that the Beachcomber was beautiful," she admitted.

"Because you were seeing it through the disinterested eyes of a kid," Duke said.

Maybe. But Alice thought it might be more than that. She'd taken the place for granted the way she'd taken her childhood home for granted. It was merely a backdrop. A setting for more important matters to take place like her first crush or her parents' divorce.

And there it was.

For Alice, the misery of her parents' divorce had cast a shadow over the Hamptons. She'd been the oldest child and the only one who remembered the incessant bickering during the marriage and the bitterness afterward. Both parents had leaned heavily on her in those early days, leaving a young Alice to cater to her even younger siblings while her parents retreated to lick their wounds. She didn't blame the setting, of course, but her negative associations endured nonetheless.

"I'd love to see you fall under its spell," Ryan said. "There's no other business like this. Not distilleries. Not farms. Nothing."

Duke waved her forward. "Come on, before you get blinded by stars in your eyes. We've got plenty of ground still to cover."

Alice's feet were sore by the time they returned to the winery. She walked everywhere in the city, sometimes thirty blocks a day when the weather was nice, so she was surprised by her body's betrayal. Middle age was a bitch.

Duke headed off to meet a friend for lunch, leaving Alice and Ryan alone in the dining area. She longed to soak her feet in a tub of warm water, but there was still more to do. Always more. It was no wonder Aunt Jean lived so long. She probably felt she didn't have a choice.

"Are you hungry?" Ryan asked.

Alice's stomach grumbled on command. "I could eat."

"Perfect. We need to sample food for the event anyway, and I thought now would be a good time."

Alice stared at him for another lingering moment. When was the last time someone asked her if she was hungry and offered to feed her? She couldn't remember. Maybe in the early days of motherhood, when she was exhausted from failed attempts at breastfeeding and delirious from lack of sleep.

Maybe then.

"Yes, that would be great," she said.

Half an hour later, they sat a small table by the window and enjoyed an expansive view of the vineyard. A silver bowl of olives rested between them, drizzled in lemon zest and oil, and Ryan had opened a bottle of cabernet sauvignon that they planned to serve at the event.

"Who plans the menu?" Alice asked. "Rosalie?"

"For the most part," Ryan said, "but Baz and I will offer input, depending on the occasion."

"How often do you host special events?"

"They tend to be seasonal. More in the summer, obviously. There's a lull until harvest season. Then the holidays. This is our slowest time of year, which is one of the reasons Jean chose it for Light Up Your Life. On certain days, we offer live music if we don't have an event scheduled."

"And who coordinates that? Wait, let me guess." Alice sipped her wine. "The events manager."

The ends of Ryan's mouth twitched. "Yes, but don't worry. That doesn't need a lot of attention. The musicians are already built into the schedule."

"So I only need to step in if there's an emergency, like one of the flute players has a blister on her lip or something."

He chuckled. "We don't often have flautists unless they're here for a wedding, but sure."

"And how many weddings are on the schedule?" Alice asked.

"For the year, or relative to your tenure?"

She fidgeted with the napkin on her lap. Just like in marriage, for better or worse, she was the owner—for now. "I guess I should know everything, right? Even if I decide to sell, having weddings already booked would factor into the value." She assumed, anyway.

"We don't need to get into the details now. You've absorbed a lot today already. Just relax and enjoy the food."

Alice couldn't set aside her worries, knowing there was work to be done. It wasn't her style. "Presumably, the events manager is the one supposed to hold the bride's hand up until the big day."

A small sigh escaped his lips. "That's usually how it works."

"Is someone doing that now?"

Ryan peered at her. "It's being handled. Think of me as Vanilla Ice."

She frowned. "The 80s rapper?"

He nodded. "If you've got a problem, I'll solve it."

She laughed. "I think you missed a 'yo' in there somewhere."

He popped an olive into his mouth. "You lost Tawny, but you've still got a team of people who want this place to succeed. You're not alone, Alice."

He was right. There was no reason to stress. The universe dealt her new cards to play and play them she shall. If she didn't crumble under the pressure of a dying husband, she'd be damned if she'd fall apart now. The only crumbling around here would involve baked apple tarts.

"Were you able to make arrangements for your kids?" Ryan asked. "I know that was a concern and, unfortunately, we draw the line at babysitting."

Alice nodded. "I asked my brother, Freddie, but he's decided to stay in the Hamptons for an extended visit, so my mom is taking them back to the city on Sunday." Alice blocked out the memory of her children's objections. Like it or not, they were going to have to take one for the team.

Ryan plucked another olive from the bowl. "I'm sorry this is wreaking such havoc on your life. I'm sure Jean didn't intend for that to happen."

"Who knows what she was thinking?" Alice didn't know her great-aunt well enough to understand her motives, so there was no point in trying.

"Look on the bright side—it might be a nice break for you and the kids. They're teenagers, right? Sometimes a little distance is healthy."

Alice didn't want to explain to Ryan that the kids were permanently distanced from their father, so the last thing she wanted to do was remove herself from the picture as well. Instead, she offered a wry smile. "My mother's presence will certainly make them appreciate me more."

Ryan laughed. "I see. She's 'that kind.'"

Alice took another sip of wine and noticed how the olives changed the way it tasted. "Do you have 'that kind' as well?"

"No, thank goodness, but I'm aware of the type."

"I fully expect to find my furniture completely rearranged when I get home." She also anticipated a constant stream of grumbling text messages from the children.

"You can threaten to rearrange hers as revenge," he said. "I assume you're staying at her house."

"That's the plan." A sense of relief permeated the statement. Not needing to share accommodation with her mother during her time here was a silver lining.

"There's a room reserved for you here, too, if you ever need to stay overnight," he said. "Jean used it on occasion, usually after a tasting or a long day."

"Good to know, thanks."

"Remind me and I'll fetch you the key before you leave today. It's for room 10."

"You'll have to tell me more about that part of the business," Alice said.

"We only have a small number of rooms, so it's not a major part of the winery, but it helps."

Alice popped another olive into her mouth and savored the taste.

"I'm glad I didn't have to do this alone," Ryan said. "Food has always been social for me. If I'm alone, I don't enjoy it nearly as much."

Goat's cheese, fig, prosciutto, gruyere, spinach...The more plates Rosalie set in front of them, the more Alice was convinced she'd died and gone to culinary heaven. The sharp and tangy flavors excited her palate and she realized it had been ages since she'd enjoyed a random assortment of food like this. Everything seemed to lose its appeal after Greg died, including meals. It didn't help that Amelia's taste buds resisted most foods that weren't fried or drenched in butter or ketchup, so Alice fell into the habit of catering to the least adventurous eater among them. Even if they ordered Japanese, Amelia rejected the sushi and would only eat miso soup or chicken teriyaki. Still, it was better than nothing.

"I guess we should talk more about the charity event," Alice said.

Ryan's eyes sparkled with amusement. "I was waiting until you had a little more to drink."

She barked a laugh. "Only if you want me to forget everything you tell me."

"This is our first year hosting Light Up Your Life," Ryan said. "That's one of the reasons there's more work involved. There's no blueprint, and, obviously, we want it to be a success for the charity."

"Which charity is it?" She hadn't thought to ask before.

"The Pancreatic Cancer Awareness Foundation."

Alice nearly spit out her wine.

"Are you okay?" Ryan asked, looking at her with concern.

Alice didn't want to put a damper on what was otherwise a pleasant lunch. "No, sorry. Just almost went down the wrong pipe."

That was the reason Ryan knew how Greg died. Aunt Jean must've chosen the charity to honor his memory. To honor Alice. She pushed aside the rising tide of emotions. Now wasn't the time to succumb to feelings.

"Tawny must've truly hated her job to leave in the middle of a new project," she said.

Hesitation flashed in Ryan's eyes and Alice recognized the

look. It was the same look Kevin Lafferty had given her two years ago when she asked about bonuses and he said he didn't get one (he did). It was also the same look Greg had given her when she asked about his test results and he said he didn't have them yet (he did).

"Tawny didn't hate it. She was just ready to move on," Ryan said.

Alice regarded him. "I feel like there's more to the story."

Loosening his tie, Ryan averted his gaze. "There's more to every story."

CHAPTER ELEVEN

ISABEL LINGERED in the kitchen of the guest house, enjoying the absence of city noises. She'd spent an hour or so in each room, imagining the possibilities. She thought it would be a good idea to tour the main house and incorporate design elements from there. Make the guest house the younger, hipper sister of the main house, but with commonalities—like she and Alice. They shared certain characteristics that connected them as siblings, but Isabel was Greenwich Village to Alice's Upper West Side.

A knock on the door cut through the quiet, startling her. She padded over to the door and cracked it open to see Mason grinning down at her. On cue, her stomach performed a somersault.

"I come in peace," he said, motioning to the slim crack.

"Sorry, city habits," she said, and pulled the door wide enough for him to enter.

His gaze flicked over her. "Your business attire looks awfully similar to mine."

She laughed when she noticed they were both wearing gray sweatpants and black hoodies. His hoodie sported the

Mets logo, whereas hers bore the one for Hamilton, the musical.

"I like to be comfortable when I'm in the zone," Isabel said.

His brow lifted. "Oh, sorry. Have I interrupted a moment of Zen?"

"Not at all. Company is always welcome." She ushered him further inside. "I've been hanging out in the kitchen, but it's time to work my way back to the living room."

"Mind if I join you? I could offer my unprofessional opinion. Maybe do a little mansplaining."

Isabel laughed. "Gee, hard to turn down such a tempting offer." She practically skipped into the living room. She tried to ignore the fact that Mason's mere presence was enough to elevate her mood.

He positioned himself in the center of the room and folded his arms. "What are we thinking? Something classy like a gilded mirror on the ceiling?"

She waved a hand at the far wall. "I'm focused on that right now. I think it would make a great feature wall."

He stroked his chin. "A feature wall. Got it. What about plaid wallpaper? Maybe red and green. It isn't just for Christmas, you know."

Isabel cast him a sideways look. "Please tell me you're joking."

Mason shrugged. "I don't know. Plaid is evergreen, isn't it?"

She made a point of not mocking other people's design choices, but *red and green plaid wallpaper*?

He cleared his throat. "Okay, I'm going to go out on a limb and say it's not." His easygoing smile suggested no hard feelings.

"Your sister has certain style preferences, in case you haven't noticed."

Mason swiveled from left to right, scrutinizing the interior. "Pool house chic?"

"Stylish and sophisticated."

Mason slid his hands into his pockets, appearing to take the information on board. "Stylish and sophisticated, huh? How about that? I still think of her as the girl who stole bowling shoes from the alley so she could wear them as a fashion statement."

Isabel burst into laughter. "Did she really do that?"

"Can you believe it?"

Isabel could believe it because she'd done the same thing in her misguided youth. Of course, Isabel retained her quirky fashion sense, whereas Brianna had clearly drifted into glossy territory.

"She changed after she got married. I don't mean in a bad way. She slowly morphed into one of those Park Avenue women, you know? All that money—how could she not?"

"For what it's worth, I like Brianna, and not just because she's a client."

Mason grinned. "Well, we have something in common then. Brianna's one of my best friends, seriously. Her hair's gotten blonder and her clothes are more expensive, but that part hasn't changed."

Isabel liked that Brianna and Mason had a good relationship, like she and Freddie. Admittedly, she wasn't as close with Finn, but he was older and a member of the Ruthie set. Like it or not, Hunton's two wives were the dividing line in the family.

"How about a white and pale blue color palette?" Mason suggested.

She gave him an approving look. "Not too bad."

"See? I pay attention."

"It's a bit played out, though," she said, and laughed when

his expression crumpled. "I'm thinking of white with gold accents."

"In the pool house?"

"The guest house," she corrected him. "A pool house conjures up images of chemicals, tubes, and a skimmer."

"You said you wanted that to be a feature wall," he said. "How does that work in a white and gold color scheme?"

Isabel spent the next hour bouncing ideas off her unqualified companion. She was surprised how much she enjoyed the back and forth. She was accustomed to working solo, perfectly content to let the ideas simmer in her head, without releasing them into the world until she was ready. And Mason wasn't as clueless as he initially seemed. His questions were insightful and Isabel found herself tweaking a few ideas in response to them.

"We've been doing a lot of talking. Can I get you a drink?" he asked.

"I'm good, thanks. You don't have to babysit me. I'm used to working alone."

Mason rubbed the back of his head. "Okay, but does that mean you prefer it? Because I'm happy to keep you company."

Usually, Isabel did prefer to work alone. She enjoyed the hum of her creative brain as she surveyed a room and put together the pieces of the design puzzle. But she couldn't bring herself to say that to Mason. The truth was she wanted him to stay.

"If you're not too busy," she said, although it occurred to her that he should be busy at this hour on a weekday. She wondered if he was both homeless and unemployed. Maybe the story about the renovated house was a lie.

He walked back to the kitchen and she followed.

"I bought a few odds and ends," she said, "but not too much."

He opened the refrigerator. "Is it too early for something bubbly?"

She laughed. "It's ten in the morning on a weekday."

He spun around holding a bottle of sparkling water. "And?"

She pounded the countertop. "Hit me, bartender."

He winked and moved to open the cabinet where he retrieved two glasses. "What's your process, aside from staring at blank walls? Do you have a list of suggestions you make for every guest house?"

Isabel splayed a hand against her chest. "Absolutely not. Half the fun is coming up with ideas while I occupy the space. I like the room to reveal itself to me."

Mason's gaze swept the interior. "What does that mean? You plan to sit and meditate in here until ideas comes to you?"

"Not quite that woo-woo, but I do feel rather than think my way through the process."

Mason gave her an appraising look as he handed her a glass of fizzy water. "I operate on instinct a lot of the time, too. I find the outcomes are better when I give myself over to it."

Isabel took a sip of water. "My oldest sister loves to make pros and cons lists for every decision. If I see one, I crumple it up and throw it away." She smiled. "Alice still hates when I do that."

"An overthinker, huh?"

"A lawyer."

Mason grimaced. "Even worse."

"What do you do for a living?" she asked.

He swallowed a mouthful of water before answering. "I'm an entrepreneur," he said.

Her eyebrow arched. "In my experience, that's code for screwing around doing nothing."

86

Mason burst into laughter. "Wow, that's direct. As it happens, I run a small angel investment company."

"So you invest in people who aren't screwing around and doing nothing."

He swilled the remainder of his water and set down the empty glass. "I'm fortunate that I can afford to be choosey."

"Is it a family business?"

"Nope. I started it with a friend of mine from business school about ten years ago. He works out of Silicon Valley and I work here."

"Why the Hamptons?" Isabel asked. Ten years ago meant that he'd set up his business before his son was born.

Mason shrugged. "Why not? It's got everything I want."

"Some would argue that Manhattan has more."

"I'm not much of a city person, although I don't mind the occasional visit. I'm basically a beach bum at heart."

Isabel placed her empty glass in the sink and turned around to assess the space.

"You've got a serious glint in your eye," Mason said. "Should I vacate the premises for a bit and give you and the room some privacy? I should hit the gym soon anyway."

"Whatever you need to do. Don't hold back on my account."

"I'll come back after my shower. I was thinking I could order us lunch, that way you don't need to stop working if you don't want to."

Isabel's stomach fluttered at the prospect of lunch alone with Mason. "Sounds good."

The moment he left, guilt began to gnaw at her. She was attracted to Mason. She shouldn't have accepted his offer. She shouldn't let him distract her while she's working either. She never would've let Jackson hang out with her while she worked. Then again, Jackson wouldn't have wanted to. He'd never taken an interest in her job. She got the impression that he secretly thought it was frivolous and unimportant, although he never said so directly.

Isabel sat cross-legged on the living room floor and tried to focus. She would have lunch with Mason, but that would be the end of it. It wasn't cheating. She and Jackson weren't even together right now. But it was only meant to be a break. A chance to regroup and come back to each other stronger than ever.

Or not.

The arrival of Mason Briggs had confused her. She couldn't let the flirtation continue. Maybe Isabel should call Brianna and tell her that she's very sorry but she can't finish the job. And then wait for the fallout. Brianna was one of her best clients with an impressive social network that extended beyond the city. Isabel would need to find new clients. The prospect was daunting, to say the least. Isabel had worked hard over the years to establish herself.

No. Everything would be fine. She could handle this. Isabel closed her eyes and tried to envision a white room with gold accents.

Mason returned an hour and a half later with a wicker basket filled with an assortment of sandwiches and snacks. "I thought we could eat outside since it's warm enough."

"Says the man who came from the gym," Isabel teased.

"No, I swear. It's downright balmy for early spring and the breeze is nonexistent."

Isabel finished typing the last of her notes on her iPad. "I'm game if you are. I spend as much time outside as possible. It helps my mood."

"Are you a SAD person?" He paused, frowning. "Okay, that came out wrong. I mean a person who suffers from

Seasonal Affective Disorder. Because there are special lamps for that, you know."

They exited the guest house and Isabel locked the door behind her out of habit.

"It's not quite to that level," she said. "Would you mind giving me a tour of the main house after we eat? I think it would help with inspiration."

"It would be my pleasure, as long as you don't tell Brianna that I'm eating and drinking in my bedroom. She hates that."

They made themselves comfortable in the lounge chairs on the airy back patio that spanned the length of the house.

Mason tapped the basket. "I didn't know what kind you'd like, so I got the variety pack."

Isabel leaned over to investigate and spotted crab salad on a croissant. "One of my favorites." She scooped it out of the basket, momentarily forgetting about Mason. Her mind went straight back to lazy summer afternoons at the beach with her siblings. Penny would pack them a picnic and tell them to get lost—so they did. They were free-range children in the best sense of the word. They'd bring pocket money for food and drinks and find ways to entertain themselves for hours.

"You look happy," Mason said, observing her. "I guess I made a good choice."

"You did." She took a bite of the sandwich and moaned with pleasure. Heavenly.

Mason appeared pleased with himself. "There's lobster roll, too." He reached into the basket and retrieved one for himself. "I'll put the rest in the fridge for tomorrow. Waste not, want not."

"I don't know," Isabel said. "If there's a second one of these, I might eat it now."

Mason's grin widened. "I won't object to seconds."

They ate in companionable silence and Isabel couldn't get over how comfortable she felt with Mason. It was as though she'd known him her whole life. After two years together, she still refused to pass gas in front of Jackson. She always left the room first or endured belly pain until Jackson left. If this were the Fifties, Isabel would be putting on her makeup early in the morning before Jackson could see her bare face.

"Tell me about this boyfriend of yours," Mason said, and Isabel's heart skipped a beat.

"How do you know I have a boyfriend?" She was certain she hadn't mentioned Jackson in their previous conversations, a fact which made her feel both guilty and uncomfortable.

Mason responded by taking a huge bite of his sandwich.

Isabel leaned back and slid a hand behind her head. "What would you like to know?"

"I don't know—the usual. Would he slay a dragon that threatened to harm you? Spend a year in a bunker with you without technology? Is he worthy of you?"

Isabel laughed. "Those are not the questions I was expecting."

"Well?" Mason chewed his sandwich, waiting.

She didn't want to reveal too much about the current state of their relationship. It felt disloyal to Jackson somehow.

"I have no complaints about Jackson. He's reliable, steadfast..."

Mason smirked. "So he's the human equivalent of a Honda."

Isabel finished the sandwich and debated whether to have the second one. She was floored that she'd already expressed the intention. It seemed a gluttonous thing to say.

"He and I make a good team," she said. Or that was what she'd believed, until the relationship started to unravel.

Mason examined her closely. "A good team? That's what I

say about Rudy. You're not in business together. You're a couple."

Isabel felt the blush creeping into her cheeks. "Jackson hates violence of any kind. He would never slay a dragon."

"Even if the dragon was about to kill you?"

Isabel shook her head. "We'd both be dead. I don't have what it takes to slay a dragon either. That would be my brother, Finn."

"Not your sister? What's her name again?" He tore open a bag of potato chips and offered her one.

"Alice." Isabel reached into the bag and pulled out a handful of chips. She was back on the beach again as a teenager, with the sun on her skin and the wind in her hair. God, how she missed those days. "Alice would want a list of pros and cons as to the best way to defeat the dragon. Then she'd want to discuss all the options before rendering her decision."

"But not Finn?"

"Definitely not. He would push his way to the front, determined to show everyone that he was capable of slaying the dragon. The more the villagers tell him it's impossible, the more he'll want to be the one to do the deed. And God forbid another person claims to be able to slay the dragon." She shook her head. "Finn would trip the other guy and make sure to kill the dragon first."

Mason chuckled. "A competitive nature. I like him already. What about the rest of your siblings?"

Isabel warmed to the game. "Chelsea would want the slaying to be perfect. She'd want to study the dragon from every angle first and decide the best place to stab him. Then she'd question her decision and wonder how she could improve her choice. Ultimately, she would delay her decision so long that the dragon would kill her first."

"Who else is there?" Mason prompted. He tossed a chip into his mouth, his eyes dancing with amusement.

"Freddie, my younger brother." She mulled over Freddie's approach to the dragon. "While Finn was pulling out his sword, Freddie would rush past us all without a weapon and try to befriend the dragon. Finn would end up saving him from certain death."

Mason crumpled the empty bag and tossed it into the basket. "Sounds like a fun family."

"We have our moments. What about you?" She turned on her side to face him. "How would you slay the dragon?

He shifted onto his back and threaded his fingers behind his head. "I'm not sure, but I do know that I'd be the body standing between you and certain death."

Isabel swallowed hard. "That's gallant of you, saving a woman you barely know."

"I told you I operate on instinct," he said.

"And?"

He didn't look at her. "And you're worth it."

CHAPTER TWELVE

Ruthie stood on the beach with her shoes off and let her feet sink into the sand. In a few hours, she'd be in the city with Keegan and Amelia. She was relieved that the timing worked out. It was April first and this short pilgrimage had been her ritual for more years than she cared to count. Counting only made her feel old, and she had enough body aches to remind her of how much she'd aged.

Indian Wells Beach was easily avoided the other three hundred and sixty-four days of the year, but not today—because this was the exact spot where she'd met the love of her life.

Carl Andrews had arrived in the Hamptons on business and brought his wife and kids to make a vacation out of it. Ruthie and her three kids were the only other people on the beach that fateful day, which wasn't surprising given the cooler temperatures. As a divorced mother of three, Ruthie had often used the beach as a playground for her trio. She'd been standing in the sand, facing the water and debating what to make for dinner, when she heard the sound of unfamiliar laughter. She'd turned and there he was. Her heart had slammed into her chest at the sight of him. Tall and broad-shouldered like Hunton, but with blue-green eyes that put the Caribbean to shame. She'd never felt such instant attraction before. Their eyes met across the beach and he'd waved, as though he were greeting an old friend.

It was Finn who ran over to meet the only other children on the beach. He'd been so thrilled to see two boys and quickly ditched his sisters. The five kids occupied each other while she and Carl engaged in conversation. His wife had stayed behind in the hotel room suffering from a migraine, so Carl had decided to get the kids out of her hair and let them blow off steam.

The hours flew by as they chatted about everything under the sun. He asked about life year-round in the Hamptons. They were from landlocked Iowa where there were lakes in abundance but no ocean. He and his wife had flirted with the idea of moving to Virginia at one point, but they'd chickened out. He'd expressed surprise that the beach was relatively empty and she'd explained the season didn't officially start until Memorial Day.

"I like the way it is now," he said, watching the waves roll in, and she agreed.

The following year Carl returned without his family. The kids had become more active in athletics and his wife decided it was best to stick to their routine. He'd looked up Ruthie's number in the phone book and called to invite her to dinner—and so began five years of the most intense and gratifying love Ruthie had ever known. That first night at the restaurant, he confessed that he'd thought about her constantly and told himself that if he ever returned, he would ask to see her again. Ruthie thought she would die right there and then, with a heart so full of happiness that it exploded, scattering shrapnel of joy in all directions. When she admitted she felt the same, they both started to cry. They spent the rest of the meal alternating between tears and laughter. Afterward, he drove her home. The kids were with Hunton, so Ruthie invited him inside, knowing that he would stay the night but wanting him to stay forever.

"What do we do?" she asked later. Her body was curled next to his, her palm flat against his chest where she could feel the thumping of his heart.

"I don't know." He closed his eyes.

"Do you love her?"

"No," he whispered. "But we have two children and I can't stop thinking that they deserve to grow up with both parents present."

Ruthie nodded. "Hunton has his faults, but he's a good father."

"And Laurie is a good mother." He rolled onto one side to look at her. "We live halfway across the country from each other. You can't leave here and I can't leave there."

"Then we'll do this," she said. "Once a year, you fly out here alone and spend the week with me."

"That doesn't sound fair to you," he said. "You deserve to meet someone."

"I did meet someone. I'm looking at him right now."

They sealed the arrangement with a kiss. Each spring for the next four years, Carl returned to the Hamptons on behalf of his tile distribution company. He was the boss, so he scheduled appointments around his plans with Ruthie. She would take the week off work, send the kids to stay with Hunton, and they'd pick up where they left off the year before.

Ruthie hadn't experienced pure joy until Carl came along. From their first meeting on the beach to their final meeting at her home. Six years total. That was all the happiness she was permitted. Once he disappeared from her life, she never felt that level of joy again. Not even when, one by one, her grandchildren arrived. Not even when the lump in her breast turned out to be benign. The joy that Carl sparked in her remained unrivaled. Sometimes she drew comfort from the memories. Other times, they overwhelmed her and dragged her into a state of despair from which she feared she'd never recover.

It still upset her that the one memento she'd possessed of their time together had vanished not long after he did—a beautiful moon shell that they found on the beach one glorious morning after a storm. They'd spotted it at the same time and both reached for it, their hands colliding. The pearlescent exterior with its purple and bronze hues had captivated them both. They'd spent the next hour talking about the life of snails and how they moved on to another shell when they outgrew their current home. The parallel to Carl's situation wasn't lost on either of them. Unlike the snail, Carl would remain in his uncomfortable shell for now. When it came time for him to leave at the end of the week, he'd placed the shell in her hand and told her to keep it safe for him so they could admire it together next year. But, of course, there was no next year.

Ruthie had maybe a dozen photos of him in total—Carl in front of the lighthouse in Montauk. Carl standing knee-deep in cold water, facing the camera, with a wave rising behind him. Ruthie always laughed at that one, remembering how shocked he'd been when the wave knocked him off his feet. As his head surfaced, she saw the huge grin on his face. The surprise hadn't rattled him or made him grumpy. She knew her response would've been different if she'd been the one standing in the water. His reaction to unexpected events was the complete opposite of hers and it was one of the reasons she fell so completely in love with him.

As much as she loved looking at the photos and reminiscing, it wasn't the same as touching an object he'd once handled and bestowed upon her as a token of his love. The loss of the shell still pained her. She'd put it on the mantle-piece, their love hidden in plain sight. Over the years, she wondered whether one of the children had gotten ahold of it and accidentally broken it. She'd even worked up the nerve to ask them about it once, but they'd seemed genuinely igno-rant of both the shell and its location.

Indian Wells Beach wasn't her only ritual. He'd once told her he made homemade waffles for his kids on Sunday mornings, so Ruthie decided to do the same—until the kids grew older and stopped rising early enough for breakfast. Sometimes she still thought of him on Sunday mornings. She pictured him in her kitchen, making waffles for the two of them and talking about their respective grandchildren. She had the grandchildren, but she didn't have Carl.

Ruthie stretched her arms and rolled her neck from side to side. Her muscles seemed to stiffen so easily now. She used to sit out here until her teeth chattered, but now she couldn't make it that long. Joint pain hit her first and that was bad enough to send her scampering indoors.

She trudged across the sand and returned to her car. An opportunistic seagull swooped low to investigate but departed when it realized she had nothing to offer.

Nothing to offer.

Ruthie's shoulders sagged. She was old, but she wasn't dead. She still mattered. She would help her daughter by going to the city with Keegan and Amelia. Carl would like that. She imagined what a doting grandfather he would've been. There were many nights when she let her mind wander. It was all too easy to picture living with Carl in the Hamptons. Her dreams were simple—arguably even dull—a far cry from the fantasy people often ascribed to affairs. Yes, there were times when the dreams were hot and heavy, but mostly they were more sugar than spice. She imagined waking up next to him each morning and greeting him with a kiss. She even imagined doing mundane tasks together like paying bills and grocery shopping. Carl had a way of making even the most basic tasks fun. During one visit, they had to fix the toilet, and she'd ended up on the floor in stitches from laughing so hard. If that had been Hunton, she would've ended up slugging him with the plunger.

Ruthie knew he would've loved her children and grand-children as much as she did. They would've loved Carl, too. As Ruthie had learned the hard way, it was impossible not to.

Freddie lingered in front of Hildreth's, debating how to spend the afternoon. The air was chilly in Southampton, not that he expected a heat wave. He wished it was summer so he could take full advantage of his free time and spend it outdoors. He pictured himself on a boat with friends, the sunshine warming his bare arms. As much as he liked the city, he missed the tranquility of the Hamptons. It wasn't some tiny island off the coast of Maine—he knew it wasn't *that* sedate—but he missed the sensation of being mesmer-ized by the sound of crashing waves. Of closing his eyes and allowing himself to be lulled into a trance. It occurred to him that he rarely smoked pot when he was here. He attributed the abstention to the close proximity of his parents, their presence still looming over him despite his age, but maybe he was mistaken. Maybe it was because he could enter the zone without artificial assistance. In the Hamptons, nature was his drug.

Freddie crossed Main Street and started back toward his car. Ideas formed with each step. Freddie never seemed able to turn off his brain. His family thought he was feckless and a little lazy, but it wasn't the truth. Freddie just had more thoughts than he could reasonably act on, but he *wanted* to embrace the constant stream of suggestions that his mind offered. His father said that Freddie had his mother's physical energy trapped inside his head. Freddie liked bringing ideas to fruition. The most satisfying feeling in the world was pushing a vision from his head into reality. Despite being the youngest of five, he'd had more jobs than any of his siblings. He'd worked for several startups, including a couple app developers. At one point, he considered opening a store right here in Southampton Village, but the high cost of rent and seasonal foot traffic put him off.

He envied Alice's inheritance. He wasn't jealous like Finn —that wasn't his way—but he wished he had a project to tackle like the Beachcomber. The winery was a Hamptons institution, but there was still room for improvement. A lot of room, in Freddie's opinion. He'd spent half the memorial service admiring the business and imagining what else he could do with it.

Freddie slid behind the wheel, his mind buzzing. The Beachcomber was only about five miles from here. He could drive over now and offer help to his sister. Why not? Alice was probably drowning in details and Freddie had two free hands and a plethora of ideas. When everyone found out that Freddie lost his job, they'd be less likely to give him a hard time. *He's been pitching in to save the family business*, they'd say. *We're so proud of him for stepping up when he didn't have to.*

He was surprised no one in his family had grilled him about his continued presence on Long Island. They seemed to accept the lame story he'd told them, except his mom, of course, who knew the truth. It helped that Freddie tended to be overshadowed by his siblings. As a result, what Freddie did or did not do was frequently overlooked.

The roads were uncluttered this time of year and it only took him about ten minutes to get there. He parked his car next to Alice's and viewed the winery with a fresh set of eyes.

He hadn't spent much time here as an adult, owing to the feud between Aunt Jean and Ruthie. He wasn't sure why a disagreement with his father's first wife should have any impact on the Penny set, but nobody asked his opinion. Ruthie was a force to be reckoned with, and his family's way of reckoning was to avoid.

There was no sign of life when he entered the winery, so Freddie wandered toward the offices.

"Can I help you?"

Freddie spun around to see the good-looking sommelier from the memorial service. His eyes widened slightly when he recognized Freddie.

"Baz, right?" Freddie said. It was hard to forget a name like Baz. Apparently, it was a nickname for Balthazar, which Freddie found equally unforgettable.

The sommelier smiled. "You're the brother."

"Freddie," he said.

"Good to see you again. Are you looking for Alice? She was in the vineyard with Duke, but I think she'll be back in a minute."

"Okay, thanks." Freddie wished he'd remembered that Baz worked here. He might've taken more care with his hair before he drove over.

"Freddie?"

He turned to see Alice coming toward him. He was wholly unprepared for the sight of his sister in a fuzzy sweater, jeans, and boots. Alice seemed to have a suit for every occasion, including Freddie's birthday karaoke party in the East Village. Her cheeks were flushed and her hair was attractively messy.

"I'm sorry. I'm looking for my sister," he said. "You may have seen her around. She looks like the corporate version of the farmer's wife in American Gothic."

Alice laughed. "What are you doing here?"

He splayed his hands. "Checking out your new venture."

"Well, it's not my new venture. It's my temporary venture until we get through this charity event and I decide what to do without everyone hating me."

Freddie suppressed a smile. "Try to contain your enthusiasm."

"Want to see my office?" Alice asked. Without waiting for his answer, she walked to the nearest door and opened it. "Technically, I stole it from Ryan, who took it from Aunt Jean. Welcome to the pit of despair."

Freddie thought the room could use Isabel's touch, but he declined to say anything negative. Alice clearly had enough on her plate without piling on.

"How's your mom doing with the kids?" he asked. "I'm sorry I couldn't help out."

"She's taking them back to the city today," Alice said, settling in the chair behind the desk. "I'm sure I'll be reading about the atrocities committed in their future autobiographies."

"Quality time with Ruthie will build their character," he said.

She motioned for him to sit in the empty chair across from the desk. "So, what's up? I doubt you came all the way over here to ask about my mom."

"I've been thinking about this place, actually." It wasn't a complete lie. He'd been thinking about for at least forty minutes.

Alice arched an eyebrow. "Let me guess—you, too, have an opinion about whether or not I should sell."

"Nope. That part's up to you. In the meantime, I'm here to offer my services."

His sister frowned. "Your services? Won't your job miss you?"

"Let me worry about that. My big sister needs a hand." He

wiggled ten fingers in the air. "And I happen to have two of them." For a split second, he thought she might cry.

"If you're serious, I would love to have you."

He shifted in the chair. Freddie had expected more resistance. "Really?"

"Yes, in fact, I know exactly how you can help." Her face brightened and Freddie recognized the look of a brilliant idea forming. It was a rare moment that he could see their similarities, but he saw it now.

"Lay it on me, sis."

"The events manager quit the day I took over and I need someone with a certain skill set." She eyed him. "Do you think you could take over until we find a suitable replacement? I don't want the whole place to go under during my brief tenure."

Freddie sympathized. It did seem unfair of Aunt Jean to place such a heavy burden on one person. On the other hand, he knew his siblings. If the older woman had left the business to all of them, there'd be more arguing than working. No, Aunt Jean had been smart to choose Alice. As the oldest and most responsible, she was the one sibling the rest of them looked up to. She'd earned their respect and he suspected Aunt Jean was banking on that fact. After all, here sat Freddie, offering his services and playing right into the old woman's hands. Freddie smiled to himself. Clever lady.

"Events manager sounds like something I can handle," he said. Of course, Freddie felt confident that he could handle anything. Someone could call and offer him the presidency and he'd just nod and start generating ideas as to how he could best fill the role.

"We have this annual charity event coming up, but that's already underway, so Ryan and I are handling it. What I need is someone to look ahead on the calendar and make sure we've got a handle on future events. I also don't want to leave huge holes in the calendar that would normally be filled."

Freddie warmed to the idea immediately. Generate new business? Yes, please.

"Are you sure you have time to devote to this?" Alice asked. "If you only have a week off, it's not going to be feasible."

Freddie rubbed his palms over his thighs. Time to come clean. "I have more than a week."

Alice was no dummy. She squinted at him. "You quit?"

"Fired," he admitted.

"This is the job Brendan got you?"

"Unfortunately. I failed a random drug test."

To her credit, she offered no judgment, only asking, "Who else knows?"

"Just my mom, but she doesn't want me to tell Dad."

Alice blinked. "Why not?"

"I think there's an issue with his heart. The doctor doesn't want him stressed."

"His heart?" Alice repeated, and Freddie saw a look of panic ripple across her features.

"It's no big deal," he said quickly. He didn't want her to worry about their dad on top of everything else. "They just want him to take it easy."

"How are we going to explain your presence after this week?"

"Let me handle it," Freddie said. "I'm not planning to keep it a secret very long. I would've told everyone by now, if my mom hadn't asked me not to."

Alice fiddled with a pen on the desk. "Well, their loss is my gain."

Freddie beamed. "Funny, that's exactly what I was thinking."

CHAPTER THIRTEEN

FINN WELCOMED the month of April with open arms. April meant a change of season and brought him that much closer to summer, the busy season for Hamptons real estate.

"What's on your agenda this week?" Jessica asked. Her desk was positioned directly across from his in the small office they shared with their administrative assistant, Beatrice. Finn regretted the decision to hire the younger woman because she seemed to spend more weekday hours out of the office than in it. Once summer rolled around, he was going to have to remedy that.

"Dr. Davis is in town," he said.

"Oh, right. How could I forget?"

Finn viewed Burton Davis as his white whale. Last summer, he spent weeks showing the cardiologist as many properties in his price range as he could find, but the good doctor couldn't bring himself to commit to one. As a person, Finn understood the mentality. After all, the purchase of a home was a big deal, especially in the doctor's price range. As a realtor, however, it annoyed the shit out of him.

Jessica nibbled on a carrot stick. "Do you think he'll see anything he likes this year?"

"He likes them all. That's the trouble."

She cut him a glance. "Okay, will he like one enough to put a ring on it?"

"He will. I've been visualizing handing him a set of keys every day for the past month." Swiveling his chair away from the desk, Finn tossed a tennis ball against the wall and caught it on the rebound.

"Finn, how many times have I asked you not to do that? It scuffs the paint."

He swiveled again to face his wife. "I just can't wrap my head around it."

Jessica sighed. "Are we talking about the Beachcomber again?"

"I'm sorry. I know I said I was done ranting."

She waved a carrot at him. "Rant away. I'm your wife. That's what I'm here for. That being said, stop torturing yourself. It's pointless and stresses you out." She paused. "And me."

"I would've been an asset." It wasn't that Finn believed his sister *wouldn't* be an asset. She was, after all, a lawyer and he could see the logic of the decision. But still. Finn was the go-getter in the family. The one with brains and balls. Alice didn't take risks. Her choices were careful and calculated. He wouldn't be surprised to learn she had spreadsheets on her computer that corresponded to all her personal decisions.

"Of course you would have," Jessica said. "I doubt Aunt Jean gave it as much thought as you're giving it now. The woman was almost one hundred years old. It was a wonder she remembered her own name."

Finn knew she was exaggerating for his benefit. Aunt Jean had been sharp as a tack, even at her age. It was one of the reasons no one had pushed her to appoint new leadership.

The Beachcomber wasn't in dire straits as far as anyone knew. No need to fix what isn't broken.

"What's going on with Mulford Lane?" he asked. "Any movement?"

"No, but it's early days." Jessica leaned against the back of her chair and gazed at him. "Why don't you tell Alice you'd like to be a part of the business? See what she says?"

Finn turned toward the wall and lobbed the tennis ball again. This time Jessica didn't object.

"It isn't realistic. We have our own business to run. Things are going well. If I have to learn the ropes at the Beachcomber, that would mean less time hustling."

"Then there's your answer. Stop stewing and focus on Dr. Davis," Jessica advised.

Finn hated that she sounded so reasonable. At least she let him vent. He was entitled to be annoyed for being passed over. He was the oldest son. Since the dawn of man, oldest sons had been the recipients of family fortunes. Sure, times had changed, but Finn had stayed here and put down roots, whereas Alice took off the second she could and rarely looked back. Why would Aunt Jean leave a beloved local business like the Beachcomber to someone who didn't even want to be here?

"Dr. Davis mentioned a private dock again," Finn said, although the necessity of a private dock seemed to ebb and flow like the tide. Sometimes it seemed like the doctor was testing him and had no intention of buying a house.

"Did you show him the house near the Shinnecock Canal? It has that amazing hundred-foot dock."

"No, it needs to be a deepwater dock or he'd have to use the marina or yacht club," Finn told her. "He's got a 37-footer." Shinnecock Canal was great for boat owners who wanted proximity to the ocean and the bay, but the dock water was too shallow to accommodate the client's yacht.

"What about those two properties in Sag Harbor then? At least one of them has a dock."

"I guess," he murmured.

"You're still stewing," Jessica accused. "I can see that muscle in your cheek twitching."

Finn bounced the ball one more time before tossing it onto his desk. He watched it roll against the lamp and wobble to a stop.

"I'll snap out of it in a few minutes."

Jessica smiled. "No, you won't, but that's fine."

A thought lingered in his mind. A reason he wasn't sure whether to say out loud because it would likely kick off a conversation he wasn't in the mood to have. In the end, he couldn't help himself. The Beachcomber decision was eating away at him and he had to scratch the itch.

"Do you think it's because we don't have kids?" Finn kept his gaze on the far wall. He didn't want to look at his wife's face and see evidence of the pain that was sure to surface.

She didn't miss a beat. "That doesn't explain why Chelsea was left out."

True. Chelsea and Brendan had three kids.

"And what about Isabel and Freddie?" Jessica continued. "They're young. There's still plenty of time for them."

Unlike us. That was the unfinished part of her statement, he knew.

Finn dared to look at his wife now. "Tomorrow, right?"

She nodded. It was the only area of their relationship where they spoke in cryptic code to each other. Tomorrow they were allowed to have sex. They'd been trying to get pregnant for three years without success. Not even a miscarriage. They were determined, though. Finn wanted a child as badly as his wife. Whatever article on conception she sent him, he read. Whatever food she cooked for him to improve virility, he ate. Whatever lovemaking schedule she set for them, he agreed to. The one thing they hadn't done was see a specialist because crossing that threshold would be an admission of defeat and neither of them was ready to wave the white flag. Finn found the idea of needing assistance with conception both insulting and demeaning. They were fit and healthy adults who wanted to conceive a child. Even better, they were achievers, the type of people who repeatedly set goals and exceeded them. They should be able to manage basic human reproduction without help.

Next year, he thought to himself. If she wasn't pregnant by her thirty-eighth birthday, then they'd schedule an appointment with a fertility specialist. But Finn didn't think the appointment would be necessary. If they just tried a little harder—if he consistently visualized a newborn in his wife's arms, he was certain they'd succeed.

Isabel studied the books of wallpaper patterns splayed across the floor of the living room. There were too many gorgeous ones to choose from—a good problem to have, she recognized.

A firm knock on the door brought her to her feet. It had to be Mason. No one else would visit her without texting first.

She opened the door and smiled. Sure enough, Mason's handsome face looked down at her.

"Hi," she said.

"Good afternoon."

A tiny thrill zipped through her as his gaze raked over her. He seemed to realize what he was doing and jerked his eyes front and center.

If he cheats with you, he'll cheat on you. Isabel was familiar with this phrase thanks to friends and many, many internet articles. But Mason wouldn't be the one cheating. She would

—technically. And she knew without a shred of doubt that she would never, ever cheat on Mason. Not that she ever envisioned herself cheating on Jackson either. Once she was with someone, she ceased to see other men in a romantic light. She knew serial cheaters—friends who had a habit of securing a new relationship before abandoning their current one. That had never been Isabel's way. Even in college, when cheating seemed like standard fare, Isabel had remained true to Rupert, her beloved British boyfriend. Rupert had returned to England after graduation and, as neither had any interest in settling in the other's home country, they'd agreed to part as friends.

"So, um. I have Asher this weekend and we were wondering if you'd like to play lacrosse with us on the beach tomorrow morning."

She leaned against the doorjamb. "You could've texted me."

"Why would I do that when you're only footsteps away?"

"I would love to, but I need to go back to the city tonight." She needed to put as much distance as possible between herself and Mason Briggs.

Mason's expression clouded over. "Big plans with the boyfriend?"

"Jackson, yes."

Mason nodded. "When are you leaving?"

"In a few hours," she said. "We have dinner reservations at Boucherie."

"Good choice. I recommend the porterhouse," he said, unsmiling.

"I'll be back tomorrow," she said, "but I have a wine tasting at the Beachcomber, so I won't be around much."

"That's the family winery?"

She nodded. "My sister's invited the family because she's

trying to work out a few kinks in the menu for an upcoming charity event and we're the guinea pigs."

"I can think of worse reasons to be a guinea pig."

She jabbed a thumb behind her. "Want to come in and help me narrow down wallpaper samples?"

He bit his bottom lip, his eyes still pinned on her. "As tempting as that sounds, I should probably go."

"I'm sorry to miss Asher," she said. "I'd love to meet him."

Mason gave her a sad smile that tugged at her heart. "Yeah, I'd like that, too."

Once Mason left, Isabel returned to the wallpaper samples and tried to focus. She couldn't let her feelings for Mason interfere with her work. It was bad enough he was Brianna's brother, but now she couldn't seem to look at a design without wondering whether Mason would like it. It wasn't that she was second-guessing her choices—Isabel was confident as a designer. It was that she wanted to *share everything* with him, from what she ate for breakfast to the burning sunset she'd spotted from the kitchen window. Everything seemed to direct her to Mason.

She flipped a page and examined more patterns. It occurred to her that she'd never once felt compelled to send a photo of a sunset to Jackson, no matter how beautiful. She'd simply admire it herself and move on with her evening. Not so with Mason. Everything Isabel saw that she liked or admired, she wanted Mason to see it, too.

She felt sick to her stomach at the prospect of seeing Jackson for dinner. She knew what she had to do, but there was more wrapped up in her decision than she cared to admit.

If only her feelings for Mason were the only secret she was carrying.

CHAPTER FOURTEEN

RUTHIE SAT on the edge of the bed in her daughter's bedroom and scrutinized the interior. There was only one framed photograph in the entire apartment—Alice and Greg flanked the children as they stood holding hands in a row under the bridge in Central Park. Their smiles seemed forced and Ruthie wondered whether they knew about Greg's diagnosis at that point. Probably.

She wandered back to the kitchen and scanned the pocket calendar she kept in her purse, counting down the days until she could return to the Hamptons. She wasn't a fan of the city. Too noisy. Too crowded. Too dirty. She couldn't understand the draw. She was surprised when Alice accepted a job in the city after law school. Ruthie thought her sensible child would bolt from the insanity at the first opportunity, but no. She wanted the prestige, Ruthie supposed, although that was more Finn's style. Then Alice married Greg, and Ruthie knew they'd take advantage of the city a bit longer. When Alice announced her first pregnancy, Ruthie waited in vain for the news that her daughter was moving closer to her family, like Renee Levin's daughter. Finally, after Greg died,

Ruthie once again assumed her daughter would flee, yet three years later, Alice was still there, raising her kids amidst the chaos. More than once she'd hinted to Alice that there was ample room for more bodies in Ruthie's house and more than once Alice refused to take the bait. Ruthie knew how to bide her time. If Harry Potter was the Boy Who Lived, then Ruthie was the Woman Who Waited.

Horns blasted outside and Ruthie closed her eyes, as though that would somehow block the sound. The selfish part of her regretted the decision to swap places with her daughter. If Ruthie ended up with a brain aneurysm, Alice would never forgive herself.

She summoned her grandchildren to the kitchen to discuss dinner options. The first thing she'd done upon arrival was place an order for delivery with the grocery store. She knew there'd be precious little in the way of ingredients in Alice's cupboards. She had a sneaking suspicion that her daughter's family subsisted on takeout and microwaveable meals.

"Can we have ramen?" Keegan asked.

"We're not having noodles for dinner," Ruthie scoffed. "That's not a meal."

"It is in Asia," Amelia said.

"Well, we're not in Asia, are we?"

Amelia leaned a hip against the counter. She was going to be tall like her father, poor thing. Tall girls tended to be awkward.

"I like mac and cheese," Amelia said.

Ruthie investigated the contents of the refrigerator to see if she had what she needed. A carton of soy milk stared back at her. She'd spotted it during her initial inventory sweep but missed the 'soy' label. She peered around the refrigerator door. "Where's the regular milk?"

"What counts as regular milk?" Keegan asked.

Ruthie rolled her eyes and shut the door. She'd have to go to the store tomorrow after the children went to school.

"Mac and cheese is out. What about meatloaf?"

"We're trying to reduce our meat consumption," Keegan said. "It's bad for the environment."

Ruthie pressed her lips together. What wasn't bad for the environment these days? Not all paper or plastic was recyclable. She wasn't supposed to eat almonds for reasons she couldn't recall. If she let all that information in, she'd end up in a guilt coma for simply existing in a world she didn't create.

"What about salmon?" she asked. "Is that allowed?"

"As long as it's responsibly sourced," Keegan said.

She folded her arms. "Should I interview the supply chain before I cook it then, just for confirmation?"

His attention shifted back to his phone and he drifted back to his bedroom.

"I like salmon," Amelia said, "but if you're going to make broccoli with it, can you steam it instead of boil it? That tastes better."

Ruthie flinched. "Why don't you get your homework done before dinner and let me worry about the cooking method?"

Amelia spun around in a half circle and disappeared from view. Ruthie muttered to herself as she pulled out a pot and pan and set to work. These two certainly had a lot of opinions for people who didn't know the first thing about cooking. She'd have to rectify that while she was here. Might as well make lemonade out of lemons. There was a lesson in that for all of them.

"Make sure you take the pans out of the oven before you preheat it," Alice had told her.

"Who uses an oven for storage?" she'd muttered, but was proud of herself for remembering.

Ruthie dutifully emptied the oven of its mismatched stack of pans before setting the temperature to 350.

An hour later, the three of them sat at the cramped circular table in the kitchen that served as the main dining area. Ruthie already missed the spaciousness of her own modest home. How did families live like this? There was no room to grow.

"Is everything to your satisfaction, lord and lady?" she asked her grandchildren.

Amelia pushed a broccoli floret with her fork, studying it. "You steamed it?"

"According to the YouTube, yes."

"It's not *the* YouTube," Keegan said.

"It's fine, Mom-mom." Amelia made a showing of stuffing the floret into her mouth and chewing.

Ruthie knew she'd overdone the steam and made the broccoli soggy, the same as when she boiled it. Really, she should just choose another green vegetable to torture.

"Put more salt on it," Ruthie said. "Salt makes everything better."

"Penny roasts broccoli like they're sprouts," Keegan said. "It's really good."

Ruthie felt her jaw tighten. "Penny is a modern marvel. No wonder your grandfather married her."

"Why didn't you remarry?" Amelia asked.

Keegan elbowed his sister. "That's rude."

"How is that rude? It's a basic question about her life. Aren't we supposed to be interested in the lives of our family members? We can't all live on our phones."

Keegan glared at his sister. "Don't make this about me."

"If the iPhone cover fits…"

Ruthie knew she had to intervene before the argument escalated. "I didn't want to marry again." While it wasn't strictly true, it was close enough to the truth.

Amelia cocked her head. "Do you like Penny?"

"Does it matter what I think?" As far as Ruthie was concerned, Penny was a fly in the ointment. She'd interfered in more family holiday schedules than Ruthie cared to count and cost her precious time with her own children and grandchildren. It also didn't help that Penny seemed to outshine her in almost every respect, including, it seemed, the cooking of vegetables.

"You answered a question with a question. That means no." Amelia seemed satisfied.

"How's the salmon? Does it taste responsibly sourced?" Ruthie asked, changing the subject. She didn't want to get in trouble later when they relayed the conversation to their mother. Alice always warned her about saying anything negative about Penny in front of the kids. A united front was apparently the key to child-rearing. If only she'd known that before she got divorced.

"It's good," Keegan mumbled.

"Well, I managed to do something right today. I'll be sure to mark this day down in history."

The kids gulped down their food at warp speed and retreated to their bedrooms. Ruthie cleared the table and cleaned up the kitchen. She was glad she didn't have to look after anyone in her everyday life. Her only wish was that she had someone to take care of her. Not every day. Just occasionally, or when she felt unwell. A nice bowl of chicken soup or a cup of tea. Then again, they might not be made to her standards and then she wouldn't enjoy them anyway. Better to do it herself and not rely on someone else who might disappoint her.

She planned to go to bed early, knowing it would be a futile gesture. Her insomnia was worse in the apartment, thanks to the incessant city noises. What did a honking horn ever accomplish?

Amelia showered first and climbed into bed with a book. "Do you know anything about zits?"

Ruthie sat on the edge of the bed and examined her granddaughter's face for any sign of blemishes. "I know that I don't want one."

"I'm getting one on my nose. I can feel the bump." She touched the slope of her nose.

"Your mother used those medicated pads for acne when she was your age. I forget the name."

"Next time you go to the store, can you get some?"

Ruthie patted the blanket over her granddaughter's leg. "Of course I can."

"Thanks. I have sensitive skin, so don't get the kind that burns."

"I won't." Despite Amelia's broccoli critique, Ruthie had no interest in inflicting pain upon her grandchild.

"We're almost out of toothpaste," Keegan said.

Ruthie twisted to look at him in the doorway. "Already? We just got here."

"It was almost empty before we left. Mom didn't have time to buy more."

The news came as no surprise to Ruthie. It sounded like Alice's schedule barely allowed her time to breathe. It was one of the reasons she'd agreed to the swap. Let Alice get a taste of life in the Hamptons without the stress of her legal work.

"Then I'll get more delivered tomorrow," Ruthie said. At this rate, she'd be on first name terms with the delivery person.

"Mom doesn't like to use the delivery service for that kind of shopping. She wants to choose everything herself," Keegan said.

"Sounds about right," Ruthie muttered.

Keegan disappeared and Ruthie glanced at the book on

Amelia's lap—*The Five People You Meet in Heaven*. "Is this for school?"

"Yes, I hate it."

"It doesn't seem particularly offensive. What's wrong with it?"

"It's boring. I don't want to read about a bunch of old white men."

Ruthie laughed. "Welcome to English literature."

"I don't connect with the material," she continued, prompting more laughter from Ruthie.

"When I was in school, it was basically Shakespeare and Dickens." That was what she remembered anyway. High school seemed a very long time ago.

"Keegan got to read *Romeo and Juliet*," Amelia said. "He says it's actually meant to be a cautionary tale."

"Is that so?" Ruthie considered his perspective. "I guess I can see his point." Love could be destructive, make people act irrationally. She knew that firsthand.

Amelia opened the book and sighed. "I wish we were reading something more exciting like *The Mortal Instruments*."

Ruthie didn't recognize the title, not that she expected to. She wasn't a big reader, probably thanks to all the Shakespeare and Dickens she suffered through in school.

"Have you set your alarm?"

Amelia tapped her phone on the bedside table. "Six-thirty."

Ruthie would've been horrified by the early start but for the fact that her insomnia would have her awake anyway. She switched off the light.

"Good night, Mom-mom," Amelia said.

"Sweet dreams."

Ruthie listened for any sound from the bathroom. Keegan was taking a long time. She tried to remember Finn at his age. Her youngest child had been obsessed with his hair. He would comb it repeatedly and then check the mirror to make sure each strand had submitted to his will.

Ruthie knocked on the door. "Are you almost finished?"

"Yes," came the muffled reply.

Ruthie thought city kids were supposed to grow up faster than those in the rest of the country, but Keegan and Amelia didn't seem particularly sophisticated to her. They just seemed like—kids, which was a good thing in Ruthie's book. She laughed to herself, remembering Keegan's remark about Alice wanting to choose her own groceries. It seemed that Alice had inherited her control issues rather than developed them independently. It was something she and Hunton fought over when they were first married. He accused Ruthie of never being satisfied with anything he did.

"Some people don't want to be happy," he'd mutter before stalking off and slamming the door. She wondered now how true his statement had been. She'd thought he was attacking her to deflect attention away from his own shortcomings. She hadn't possessed the self-awareness to consider that maybe—just maybe—he had a point.

CHAPTER FIFTEEN

ALICE BUSTLED INTO THE KITCHEN, her frayed nerves beginning to show. She was accustomed to working somewhat independently, with occasional input from a partner or assistance from a paralegal. The Beachcomber, on the other hand, was purely a collaborative effort.

"How are we doing, Rosalie?" she asked.

The chef glanced up from the work station. "Same as we were the last five times you asked me."

"Has it only been five?" Alice asked. "I thought this might be lucky number seven."

Rosalie continued chopping peppers, her feathers unruffled. Alice was usually the one with a knife in a steady hand. It felt strange to be on the other end for a change.

"We've been doing this for a long time, Alice," Rosalie said. "Trust us to do it right."

Ryan tapped the proposed menu in his hand. "To be fair to Alice, this is our first time hosting this event."

Henri and Baz entered the kitchen, each carrying a crate of wine bottles. "I think you'll find that new territory is where I excel," Henri said.

"And I think you'll find it's where I don't," Alice shot back. At least she was aware of her weaknesses. That was half the battle, or so they said.

"It's only your family coming tonight for the tasting," Baz said, setting the crate on the counter. "What's the worst that can happen?"

Laughter erupted from the opposite end of the kitchen and Freddie emerged from the shadows. "Word to the wise—keep the sharpest knives in the kitchen."

"Okay, they're not *that* bad," Alice said.

"Wait until wedding season starts and then you'll see some real family drama." Rosalie shook her head. "People talk about Bridezillas, but MOBs are the worst in my book."

"MOBs?" Freddie asked. He wandered over and tried to steal a sliver of red pepper from the chopping board, but Rosalie's menacing look stopped him cold.

"Mother of the Bride," Alice said, holding back a laugh. Clearly, Rosalie wasn't going to be as easily charmed by Freddie as other mortals.

"I spoke to one of the brides yesterday to let her know I'd be taking over for Tawny and she sounded great," Freddie said. "Very bubbly."

Rosalie and Baz exchanged glances. "That must be Francie," Baz said. "Bubbly is the best word to describe her."

Freddie's head bobbed up and down. "Yes, Francie's her name."

"Francesca is lovely," Rosalie said. "It's Josephine you need to watch out for."

"Josephine is the MOB, I take it," Alice said.

"Oh, yeah." Rosalie angled her head toward Freddie. "You're going to have your work cut out for you with that one."

"I didn't even realize the Beachcomber was available for

weddings until you told me," Alice said. "Shows how much I've paid attention."

"The weddings started about ten years ago," Ryan said. "Most of the other wineries were offering wedding packages by that point, but Jean was resistant."

"She worried that the wine would become secondary and the quality would suffer," Henri said, "which I respect."

"What changed her mind?" Alice asked.

"The great motivator—money. This place wouldn't have been able to stay afloat without special events. It's that simple." Ryan set the proposed menu for Light Up Your Life on the counter. "This next event might be for charity, but it's good for business all the same."

Rosalie smiled. "With the added benefit of no MOB."

"At least my mother isn't here," Alice said.

"Amen to that," Freddie chimed in.

Ryan placed a hand on each of her shoulders and looked her in the eye. "Relax, Alice. Everything will be fine. It's only a tasting." He gave her shoulders a quick squeeze before releasing her.

Alice smoothed a wayward strand of hair. "All right. If everything's under control in here, I'm going to freshen up before the invasion."

She'd deposited a change of clothes and toiletries in room 10 so that she didn't need to drive back to her mother's house before the tasting. She really wanted the evening to go smoothly and for her family to see the Beachcomber was in good hands.

As she exited the winery and headed toward the separate row of lodging, a wave of panic began to rise, threatening to overtake her. She wanted to get lost among the vines and scream at the top of her lungs. Why did Aunt Jean add this stress to her life? And why did she agree to stay at all? She shouldn't have succumbed to family guilt. She was forty-eight, old enough to set her boundaries and stick to them, yet here she was—upending her life to please who exactly?

For the next hour, she shut herself away in room 10 and tried to focus on the positives as she made herself presentable. The Beachcomber staff was great. Tawny's departure aside, they'd pulled together and made every effort to ease Alice into the business. Ryan, especially.

Staring at her reflection in the bathroom mirror, Alice noticed the color in her cheeks deepen at the thought of Ryan. Quickly, she glanced away from her reflection. Ryan McElroy was the general manager. It was his job to oversee the transition and make sure Alice knew everything there was to know about the Beachcomber. Nothing more. Just because she thought he was handsome…

Alice exited the bathroom, refusing to indulge the thought. She hadn't looked at a man through a romantic lens since Greg died and she had no interest in starting now. Aunt Jean left her the Beachcomber, not an eligible bachelor.

She combed her hair one more time, grateful that her mother wouldn't be here tonight to comment on it. No matter how much care she took with her appearance, she could count on Ruthie for an offhand comment about how she must've driven with the window down or come straight from the office.

As she made her way back to the winery, she passed Henri outside.

"You look lovely, Alice." With his slight accent, he pronounced her name like Elyse, but she didn't mind.

"How's everything going?" she asked.

"Excellent. Duke and I finished a walk-through of the vineyard earlier to see if any vines looked thirsty. It's been a bit of a dry spell."

"Anything to be concerned about?"

"Not at all. Enjoy the tasting. I'll be sampling barrels and doing blending trials tomorrow. You should join me. I think it will be of interest to you."

"That sounds great, thanks." More to learn. There was a time in her life when she enjoyed learning. Why did she stop?

"I noticed a car in the parking lot," Henri said. "I think some of your family might have arrived."

Alice's head swiveled to the winery and her heart began to beat rapidly. "It's going to be fine," she said, more to herself.

"That's the spirit. Jean is cheering you on from the heavens."

Alice wasn't convinced. Sometimes it felt like Aunt Jean was spitting on her from above.

She drew a deep, cleansing breath and headed toward the entrance to the winery where she immediately ran into Isabel.

"I'm so excited for this," Isabel said. "I'm glad you invited everyone."

"Light Up Your Life was Aunt Jean's project, so it feels right that we should all play a role in pulling it off." Her phone beeped with a text message from Amelia, asking for the location of the extra phone charger because Keegan lost his. Alice released a gentle sigh and typed a response—*In the drawer closest to the fridge.*

"Is your mom handling everything okay in the city?" Isabel asked. "Sorry, I saw Amelia's name."

She offered a wan smile. "No one's complaining." Much. "I'm seeing them soon for a quick visit. I promised Amelia."

"You won't be here for very long in the grand scheme of life," Isabel said. "And I'm sure this is a nice break for you." Her brow creased as she seemed to realize the absurdity of her statement. "Okay, *break* was probably the wrong word to use."

Alice laughed. "You got that right." But Isabel was right.

This was a break from her normal routine and, even though she was incredibly busy, there was value in that.

Together, they entered the winery and she spotted Finn and Jessica. That they were the first to arrive came as no surprise to Alice. They liked to be first in everything, including arrivals and departures. She could already see her brother scoping the room to see whether any potential clients lurked in the shadows.

"It's just family tonight," Alice said. "We'll have a big crowd for Light Up Your Life, though, so mark your calendar."

"If you need me to get the word out locally, let me know," Finn told her.

"Absolutely," Alice said. "I'll give you all the details before you leave."

Freddie entered the room, deep in conversation with Baz, and Alice hoped there wasn't a problem. Before she could ask, her father arrived hand-in-hand with Penny, and Alice felt a wave of tenderness wash over her. What was it like to be over seventy and still want to hold hands with your spouse? She'd never know now.

Chelsea and Brendan were the last to arrive, which was also not a surprise to Alice. Between their three kids and Chelsea's perfectionist tendencies, the Somers family was habitually late to everything. Alice suspected that her sister changed her dress at least three times before Brendan insisted they leave the house.

"You look beautiful," Alice said, and kissed her sister's cheek.

"I told her that the first two times," Brendan said.

"Third time's the charm," Chelsea said meekly.

Isabel hugged her. "I'm so glad you're here. It's nice to be together again so soon, and not because someone died."

"Technically, this is still because someone died," Brendan said. "The same someone, in fact."

Chelsea gave her husband an exasperated look. "This should be fun." Chelsea turned toward Alice. "Right? This is a fun thing."

"Yes, definitely," Alice said. "We're sampling food and wine and making decisions on which ones to include for the event. All we'd like is your feedback. Ryan has cards for everyone to complete before you leave."

"Ryan?" Chelsea asked. "He's the tall, good-looking one in the suit?"

Alice felt her cheeks burn and hoped no one noticed. "The one in the suit, yes," she said.

Isabel had looked forward to the tasting all week, but now that she was here, she felt like going back to the guest house and climbing under the covers. Last night with Jackson had been difficult and she couldn't seem to focus on anything for more than thirty seconds without thoughts of Mason pushing their way to the forefront. She didn't tell anyone that she'd gone to the city last night because it would raise more questions than she cared to answer.

"Let's join the others," Alice said, and started toward the table.

It was only when walking behind Alice and admiring her calves that Isabel realized her sister was wearing a dress. It was pretty and stylish, something Isabel might've chosen for herself.

"I love that dress," Isabel said.

Alice paused and waited for Isabel to fall in step. "Thanks. I did a little shopping the other day. Thought I'd do my bit to support local businesses."

"Oh, I see. Generating goodwill now that you're also a

local business owner." And here she thought Alice had taken renewed interest in her reflection. Too bad. Isabel would like to see her sister back in the dating pool.

"There's an empty seat waiting for you," Freddie said.

Isabel spotted the empty chair between Freddie and Jessica. She smiled at the assembled guests and gracefully took her seat.

"You look gorgeous," Jessica whispered.

Isabel mouthed 'thank you.' Jessica's compliments tended to stem from a place of envy and competition and Isabel had no interest in feeding her sister-in-law's weak spot. Whereas Alice and Chelsea praised her choices with a loving eye, Isabel sensed the silent judgment and criticism that accompanied praise from Jessica.

Once everyone was seated, the general manager approached the table with a friendly smile. "Thank you all for coming tonight. I'm Ryan McElroy. I met some of you at Jean's memorial service. She would be so pleased to see you back so soon to help us choose our menu for her pet project, Light Up Your Life." He rested a hand on Alice's shoulder at the head of the table. "I'm happy to report that Alice has been making Jean proud. She's fully immersed herself in the business and we're thrilled to have her."

Isabel observed Alice as she tilted her head back to smile at Ryan. There was a spark between those two, she felt it in her bones. She looked around the table, wondering whether anyone else noticed, but they seemed oblivious.

Next, the sommelier introduced himself and Isabel listened attentively as he launched into a description of the wines they'd be tasting this evening. Isabel wasn't fussy about wine and looked forward to trying each one.

"It's essential to expectorate," Baz said, "which is why you'll each find a paper cup as part of your place setting."

"Swirl, sniff, sip, swish, and spit," Alice interjected.

"It helps to make notes after each one so you don't confuse them later," Baz said.

"I'll confuse a lot of things later after too much wine," her father interjected with a laugh.

A server appeared carrying two plates of food and set one at each end of the long table.

"We'd like notes on the food, too," Ryan said. "If there are two items you think work exceptionally well together, let us know. Same if you dislike something. Please don't be shy. We want this to reflect your tastes as a family."

"I feel so special," Penny said, as Baz went around the table pouring wine into their glasses.

Isabel marveled at the food options as the server continuously returned to the table with additional plates. Tapas dishes, a selection of cheeses, bruschetta, a mezze board, a vegetable platter—Isabel was in her element. For a brief moment, she felt envious of her sister. She wanted to trade her wallpaper samples for Beachcomber samples.

"You're supposed to spit, remember?" Jessica whispered to her.

Isabel was enjoying the wine so much that she'd forgotten.

Freddie leaned over and said, "Waste not, want not."

"What's going on with you, Freddie?" Jessica asked. "I was surprised when Finn said you were still in the Hamptons."

"This seems like the place to be right now for members of the Hughes family," Freddie said, "and I am such a member."

Isabel glanced at Brendan to see if he'd overheard, but, thankfully, he was engaged in a discussion about basketball with her dad.

Despite her repeated attempts to spit, Isabel's head began to buzz from the effects of alcohol. She knew she wasn't the only one—Jessica always got louder when she drank too much. Isabel had once calculated a ratio of one decibel per drink for her sister-in-law.

Freddie knocked on the table. "Finn, you're going to have to carry your wife into the house tonight if she keeps sampling." He used air quotes around 'sampling.'

"I guess all that wine means Jess isn't pregnant," Brendan said. The table fell silent and Brendan looked around, confused. "What? I thought that was a good thing. It's not like these two high fliers want to be saddled with kids."

Chelsea handed her husband her own glass of wine. "Here. Keep your mouth occupied, sweetheart."

"What? I don't get it." Brendan focused his attention on Finn and Jessica. "Back me up, guys. If you wanted kids, you'd have them by now."

Isabel observed her brother-in-law's flushed face and realized, he, too, had done his share of swallowing tonight.

Chelsea pressed her shoulder against her husband's. "It's none of our business, so please stop talking about it."

Brendan picked up the wine glass in front of him and tipped it back, polishing it off in one gulp. "Listen," he began, setting down the glass.

"I lost my job," Freddie blurted.

Everyone turned to stare at Freddie.

"The job Brendan arranged for you?" Chelsea asked.

"I'm sorry, Bren," Freddie said. "If it's any consolation, it wasn't a performance issue. It was stupid bureaucracy, but the good news is that it freed me up to help Alice here at the Beachcomber."

Isabel's mother looked pained. "Now isn't the time for this, Freddie."

Her father seemed to have a delayed reaction. "What happened? Freddie's working here now?"

"Alice needed a new events manager, so I offered to fill in

until the Beachcomber's fate has been decided." Freddie ended the statement with a dramatic dun-dun-dun that no one seemed to find amusing except a drunken Brendan, who barked a laugh.

"I never liked that guy anyway," Brendan declared. "He was a complete tool in college. I only talk to him because he gets good seats for all the games."

Inwardly, Isabel felt relieved. She didn't want the news to kick off a feud. She glanced at her father and tried to gauge his reaction.

"Well, I guess if we're in confession mode, I have news," her father said. "It's no big deal, so I don't want anyone to be concerned, but I have angina."

Brendan's cough was mixed with laughter. "You have a what?"

Chelsea whacked him between the shoulder blades. "*Angina*, Brendan. Unclog your ears."

"I'm not on any meds," her father continued. "Just aspirin."

"And we'd like to keep it that way." Her mother stroked his arm in a gesture that struck Isabel as both affectionate and protective. They were the real deal, her parents.

"We've started doing yoga at home, too," her father said. "It's been challenging, but I think it'll be good for me."

Isabel suddenly felt lightheaded. She knew she shouldn't have finished that last glass of wine. Wordlessly, she pushed back her chair and headed to the restroom for a few minutes of peace and quiet in which to process the news. Pressing her forehead against the cool metal door, she stood in the stall for what seemed like an eternity. She didn't hear the restroom door swing open, only the sound of her sister's voice.

"Isabel, are you in here?" Chelsea called.

"Yes. I'll be out in a minute."

"Are you feeling okay? Freddie said you might've had too much to drink."

"I'm fine." Isabel emerged from the stall door and met her sister at the sink.

"You don't look fine. You look upset."

Isabel couldn't meet her sister's gaze, not even in the mirror's reflection. "Nothing I can't handle. You don't have to worry about me."

Chelsea enveloped her in a hug. "I know I don't have to worry about you, but I will anyway. You're my baby sister."

Isabel fought the urge to cry into the soft material of Chelsea's sweater, but she had too much respect for cashmere to water it with her salty tears.

"Is it Jackson?" Chelsea prodded. "Did you two have a fight?"

Isabel disengaged from her sister's embrace. "Not a fight, no. We're just...I ended things."

"Because of something he did?"

Her throat thickened. "No, because of me."

To her credit, Chelsea didn't pry further, although Isabel didn't expect anything less. Chelsea and Alice weren't gossips, which was more than Isabel could say for their mother. Even Isabel's own mother was susceptible to fishing out information solely for the sake of it, which was the main reason Isabel didn't confide in her. Penny would feel compelled to tell Hunton and then Isabel's father would look at her with the disappointment he generally reserved for Freddie. Isabel didn't want to be the new Freddie.

"Can you fix it?" Chelsea asked. In a maternal gesture, she swept back a few strands of Isabel's hair that were sticky with tears.

"I could." Isabel paused to draw breath. "Only I don't want to."

Chelsea pressed her lips together in a thoughtful gesture. "I see."

Isabel pulled a paper towel from the dispenser and wiped her face. "How did you know Brendan was the right guy for you?"

A dreamy smile touched her sister's lips. "I don't know that I could identify the exact moment. I can only say that I don't remember a time when I *didn't* think he was the right guy, if that makes sense."

Isabel reflected on the first time she met Jackson. There'd been nothing romantic about their interaction. He was at the same party in the city, thrown by mutual friends. They'd talked within a smaller group and found common ground. He asked her out that night and she said yes. In the subway on the way home, she'd felt...pleased. Not excited or elated but pleased. She remembered wanting to feel more, but she knew she had a tendency to romanticize things and put the idea out of her head. There was nothing wrong with Jackson. She was thirty-four at the time. If she hadn't found the man of her dreams by then, she thought maybe it was because her expectations were unrealistic.

"Jackson is a good person," Isabel said.

"Of course he is." Chelsea clasped her hand. "Stop feeling guilty. Just because he's a good person doesn't mean you have to stay in a relationship with him. You're under no obligation to make yourself unhappy in order to avoid making a good person unhappy."

Isabel felt the pressure of tears returning. She had to cut off the conversation before it overwhelmed her. The last thing she wanted was for her family to see her in a state of distress. They'd pepper her with questions for the remainder of the evening and Alice's tasting would be ruined.

"I haven't swallowed any wine tonight," Chelsea said. "Do you want me to drive you back to the guest house? That's where you're staying, right? I'll come back here for Brendan. He's too drunk to care."

Isabel nodded. "If you don't mind. I'll get my car tomorrow." Her departure might raise questions, but at least they'd have to wait until later to ask them.

The sisters returned to the table where Isabel feigned a headache and thanked Alice and the rest of the staff for a wonderful evening.

"How's the project coming along?" Chelsea asked on the drive to East Hampton.

"Great, actually. I didn't expect to enjoy it as much as I am."

Chelsea laughed. "It is a pool house, right?"

"A guest house, technically," she said. "There are living accommodations. It's bigger than my apartment."

"You said the client's in the city, though, right? That probably helps you work faster."

Isabel leaned her head against the passenger side window, watching the lights as they passed by. "Mason, Brianna's brother, has been staying there. In the main house, not with me in the guest house. He's been good company."

Chelsea tossed her a knowing look. "Mason, huh? And does this Mason have anything to do with your breakup with Jackson?"

"Yes and no." It wasn't as simple as that, but Isabel couldn't bring herself to get into the details. Not when she didn't want to face them herself.

"You can talk to me about anything," Chelsea said. "You know that, right? No judgment."

"I know." But Isabel wasn't ready.

As Chelsea pulled into the driveway, Isabel noticed all the lights were off in the main house and she breathed a sigh of relief. She didn't want to see Mason right now. Her head was starting to throb and she wanted nothing more than to crawl under the covers and forget her life for a little while.

Chelsea whistled. "Holy smokes. This place is insane. Finn would sell his soul to get a listing like this."

Isabel cracked a smile. "He and Jessica both." She popped open the passenger door. "Thanks for taking care of me tonight."

"Anytime, I mean it."

Isabel smiled at her sister. "I know you do. Go easy on Brendan later. He's just having fun."

Isabel took her time walking around the house to the backyard, breathing in the fresh air and admiring the blanket of stars above. When she was younger, she and Freddie would sit in their backyard and try to count them all. She missed the simplicity of those days.

"Isabel?"

Her heart stopped. Slowly, she turned to see Mason seated in one of the lounge chairs on the patio.

"What are you doing out here in the dark?" she asked.

"Waiting for you." He rose from the chair and walked toward her. "I wanted to talk to you."

She took a step backward. "Now's not a good time."

"I can't stop thinking about you," he said.

"Distract yourself," she said. "That's what I've been doing." She realized it was the first time they'd openly acknowledged their connection. "Read all the Harry Potter books. Watch all three Godfather movies. Run a marathon on the treadmill."

"You think I haven't tried?" His voice cracked with emotion and he didn't seem remotely embarrassed by it.

Isabel felt torn between rushing into his arms and running away. Yes, she'd ended things with Jackson, but there were other considerations. Maybe she could hide in the dunes until he gave up the search and went to bed.

Bed.

She wanted Mason in her bed. She wanted him more than anything in the world.

"Do you love him?" Mason asked. "Because if you do, I'll walk into the house right now and leave you be. I swear it."

Isabel studied the walkway beneath her feet. "I thought I did."

"And now?"

She lifted her face and met his hopeful gaze, her heartbeat thundering between her ears. "Now I know that being very fond of someone isn't the same as love."

"Is that why you met him for dinner last night? To tell him?"

"Yes," she said, so softly that she barely heard her own voice.

They stared at each other for an extended moment. She'd never felt such longing for a man and the depth of her feelings terrified her.

Later, she couldn't remember which one moved first. She only remembered their lips crushing together in desperation. In one fell swoop, he scooped her off the ground and carried her into the guest house. They didn't make it to the bedroom. They made love on the sectional sofa that Isabel would soon be replacing with a white Chesterfield-inspired sofa with tuxedo arms. Afterward, Isabel rested her head on his bare chest and listened to his heartbeat. The world had tilted on its axis, but she'd never felt more grounded.

So this is what love feels like, she thought.

She was more than pleased.

CHAPTER SIXTEEN

DESPITE A THROBBING HEAD, Chelsea sat in front of her computer the next morning, fully intending to finalize her article. It didn't take too much wine to trigger a headache. She resented her body's response to even trace amounts of alcohol. She seemed to suffer the consequences without reaping the benefits. According to her doctor, she had peri-menopause to thank for that.

At least she was alone. Now that the kids were older and disinterested in toys, Chelsea was able to claim the old play-room as her office. She only worked in there when the other members of the family were home, though. On a regular weekday, Chelsea preferred to sit at the table in the kitchen because it was the room with the best natural light. Her envi-ronment made a difference to her ability to work. It came from a place of privilege, she knew. She highly doubted Charles Dickens had needed the light 'just so' before tackling *Great Expectations.*

Chelsea fixed a typo and skimmed the paragraph for more errors. The article was about father-and-son pilots who offered flights between the Hamptons and New York

City. Chelsea had interviewed the duo three weeks ago and had amassed all the information she needed, but she was struggling to finish the article to her satisfaction. She suspected it was the subject matter, although that didn't explain her heel-dragging in relation to the other dozen articles where she'd missed deadlines.

Chelsea reread the part of the article where the son talked about getting his pilot's license at the tender age of eighteen. His father had planted the seed at a young age, and what little boy didn't dream of taking to the skies one day? Some families bonded over baseball or golf. These two bonded over airplanes. It came as no surprise that the son was still single, despite being a pilot and running a successful business. He likely had no room in his heart for anything other than flying the friendly skies. Chelsea tried to keep her mind from wandering into the past, but it was no use. It was impossible to write an article about a dashing pair of pilots without remembering Fuller Bairstow.

When Chelsea was eighteen she fell in love, only the feeling wasn't reciprocated. Fuller's love was airplanes and Chelsea had arms of flesh and bone where wings should be. Like the men in the article, Fuller's father was a pilot and he was determined to follow in his footsteps. He'd even entertained the idea of becoming an astronaut, which ignited Chelsea's own dreams and desires. If Fuller could become an astronaut, why couldn't she become a writer? Yes, she knew there had to be janitors and cashiers, too—a point her parents had driven home many times over the years—and maybe she'd end up in a job like that, but Fuller unleashed the possibility that maybe—just maybe—Chelsea could be exactly who and what she wanted.

"How's my beautiful wife?"

Chelsea had been so lost in her thoughts that she hadn't heard him enter the room. Brendan stood behind her chair and wrapped his arms around her. She inhaled the familiar scent of musk and mint. He always brushed his teeth as soon as he woke up and showered after breakfast. She only brushed her teeth after breakfast. If she brushed before she ate, it triggered her nausea button. She didn't understand the point of brushing beforehand anyway, but it was the kind of thing that didn't warrant a discussion. Brendan was a grown man, a wonderful husband, and an amazing dad. If he wanted to brush his teeth before breakfast, so be it. If anything, he had a right to complain because he had to endure her morning breath. The fact that he liked to kiss her anyway suggested he didn't consider it a hardship.

"Eggs?" she asked.

"I can make them."

Brendan was great about shouldering half the domestic load, or at least as much of it as his schedule allowed. Laundry, cooking, food shopping, taking two moody cats to the vet, and chauffeuring children to various activities were all part of their routine. Chelsea knew she'd chosen her partner wisely. She wasn't as organized and hardworking as Alice, so Chelsea needed someone who offset her deficits. After Greg died, Chelsea went through a period of anxiety about losing Brendan. She knew she wouldn't lean into the role of head of household as easily as Alice had. She suspected that Alice found basic tasks fulfilling and, although Chelsea understood that satisfaction in the mundane, she didn't feel it herself. She was bored by household chores and easily distracted by the call of something more creative. If there were counters to wipe down and a dishwasher to load, you could bet Chelsea would find a way to turn a smattering of breadcrumbs into a story in her head and forget all about the task at hand. Daphne was now at the age where she noticed the breadcrumbs and other maternal failures, and Chelsea was thankful that her daughter didn't needle her about them. If Daphne saw crumbs, she simply swept them away without the need to criticize. Chelsea knew snarky teenagers existed, but she was grateful not to be raising one—not yet, anyway. There was still ample time for Ava and Daniel to turn against her.

Her phone lit up with a text and she glanced at the screen, inwardly groaning when she saw her editor's name.

Are we still on target for tomorrow?

No, Chelsea thought. She wasn't happy with the words she'd written and wanted to give the article another pass.

What time again? she wrote. Even her stalling tactics were terrible. Face it, she sucked at writing. What made her think she could do this professionally?

The sooner the better but no later than 5.

Chelsea felt the familiar tendrils of fear crawling through her stomach. Forget hot flashes, the pressure of a deadline made her break into a sweat. She responded with a thumbs up emoji and turned the phone facedown so she didn't see any more incoming text messages.

Brendan's gaze flicked to her face. "Was that Ed?"

She nodded. "I need to polish my piece today."

"You've been working on that article like it's the Gettysburg Address. Just finish it. There are no lives hanging in the balance."

Chelsea's shoulders tensed. She didn't need her husband to give her a hard time. She knew the article was taking longer than it should. She also knew she'd blown past the two most recent deadlines and that she couldn't afford another delay or she'd be out of a job.

"Maybe you'd like to finish it for me?" she asked in a neutral tone. Even with three kids, Chelsea rarely raised her voice. It wasn't her style. Her mother had been loud throughout her childhood and the sound only made Chelsea shrink until she disappeared.

Brendan squeezed her shoulders. "Nobody wants that. There's a reason I have an assistant who writes my letters for me."

She reached for his hand and held it for a minute, relishing the skin-to-skin contact. Brendan's presence was often enough to calm her, but touching him was even better. He was solid yet soft, and she was grateful for him.

From a distant room, one of the kids yelled for her.

"I'd better get started on breakfast before the mutiny kicks off." He kissed her cheek and left her alone to work.

The moment he left the room, Chelsea's thoughts returned to Fuller. He died not long after his twenty-first birthday, when his small plane crashed not far off the coast, cutting short a life full of potential. A part of Chelsea died that day, too. She'd been clinging to the possibility that someday, when they were both older and wiser, Fuller would realize what he'd been missing and make room in his life for more than airplanes. Fuller's death forced her to let go of hope and that early life lesson changed her. She shut down, closing herself off from emotional connections, until love became a window too small to climb through. She'd remained rooted in place, able to observe and acknowledge its existence without allowing herself to fully experience it. Then she met Brendan and, ever so slowly, the window expanded to the size of a door large enough to walk through. So she did.

Finn paced the length of the patio, waiting for his client to emerge from the house with a verdict. Dr. Davis was back in the Hamptons to find his dream house and Finn hoped this East Hampton beach house would be the winner. Finn had already escorted him through all seven-thousand square feet and now Finn was giving the doctor space to wander on his own.

The pool water looked cloudier than he would've liked. Finn had suggested that the owners open it early, explaining that an open pool looked much more appealing to buyers than one with a cover. It seemed they'd followed his advice but hadn't been diligent about monitoring the water.

His phone pinged with another text from Jessica, asking for an update. He silenced the phone as Dr. Davis appeared.

"What a house," the doctor said.

Finn couldn't interpret the doctor's tone, which was unsurprising. Part of his job likely demanded that he sound calm and put his patients at ease, even when the news was grim.

Finn clapped his hands together. "What do you think? Amazing, right?"

"How do we get to the beach?"

"Right this way."

They left the backyard and followed the path to the beach. The salty air filled Finn's nostrils and he immediately felt invigorated. One of the reasons he loved his job was this moment right here—walking from the serenity of a backyard straight to the beach to listen to the sound of the waves. He didn't even mind the occasional mark of a seagull. It was a worthy trade.

"Bit of a walk," Dr. Davis said. "And no water view."

"I can find one closer." It would cost more, of course, but Dr. Davis didn't seem bothered when Finn showed him properties slightly above his proposed budget. Some clients told him right away that they did not, under any circumstances, want to see a property outside of their budget. They didn't want to fall in love with something out of their reach. Finn understood that—but Dr. Davis wasn't one of those people.

"No rush," Dr. Davis said. "You know I'm willing to wait for the right thing." He cast an appraising glance at Finn. "Besides, I think we both look ready for a rest. Marcie and I stayed out too late with friends last night. What's your excuse?"

Finn chuckled. "This is what happens after forty. You can't hide your hangovers. Jess and I were at the Beachcomber. It's a winery in Southampton. My sister's the new owner."

Dr. Davis grunted his approval. "Wow. Good for her. That can be a tough business."

"She didn't exactly choose it. Our Aunt Jean was the owner, but she died recently and left it to Alice."

Dr. Davis rubbed his forehead with his thumb, which gave Finn the impression that he was grinding the information into his brain. "Your aunt left the winery to your sister but not to you?"

"Jean was my father's aunt. She had no kids of her own, but she wanted to keep the business in the family."

"Yes, but why not leave it to you, too? You obviously have a good head on your shoulders."

Finn appreciated the compliment. "My dad has five kids," he said. "I think she might've been trying to prevent infighting."

"I see," Dr. Davis said, in a voice that suggested he did not.

"I like what I do," Finn said. "I don't need the Beachcomber." The comment sounded more flippant than he intended. He needed to stop talking about it or he risked sounding like a spoiled brat in front of his client. It was unprofessional and Finn prided himself on being professional at all times.

"It's nice to be passionate about your job," Dr. Davis said. "We should all be so lucky."

Finn motioned to the beach. "Speaking of lucky, want to feel the sand in your toes?"

Dr. Davis laughed as he slipped off his loafers and socks. "I feel obligated."

They wandered closer to the water with the hem of their trousers rolled up. Finn never tired of the water. His father used to joke that Finn's veins pumped saltwater instead of blood.

"My father was a doctor," Dr. Davis said. "Have I mentioned that?"

"No, sir. You haven't." Finn joined him in the surf. Sunlight shimmered on the water and Finn pretended it was eighty degrees outside.

The doctor removed his glasses and wiped the lenses with the hem of his shirt. "Dad was an OB. Had his own practice in St. Paul."

"Minnesota?"

"That's right. I grew up there. Went to the University of Iowa for med school, just like him."

"I'll bet that made him happy."

Dr. Davis grunted. "You would think. He was happy up until the point where I announced I wanted to do cardiology. You would've thought I'd announced I was joining the circus."

Finn scratched the back of his neck. "He was that upset?"

"He had a vision of the future, you see. An expectation. And in a single moment, I crushed his hopes and dreams of taking over his practice."

Finn knew there was more to the story. He'd spent enough time with the doctor to know that his tales always had a point. "Let me guess. You have a brother."

Dr. Davis smiled at him. "A sister. Miriam's two years younger. She also attended medical school."

"And became an OB."

Dr. Davis smiled. "You're a smart guy, Finn. One of the reasons I like you." He watched as the gentle waves rolled toward them. "Miriam was so excited to tell our parents about her decision. Once the cat was out of the bag, she waited patiently for our father to invite her to join the practice."

"But he didn't?"

"Nope. Miriam acted like she didn't care, but my mother and I knew better. Miriam was hurt, understandably so."

"Did your father ever say why?"

"Not to her, but he told me." Dr. Davis blinked away the bright sunlight. "Let's just say my old man was a remnant of his time."

"He didn't want to bring Miriam into the practice because she's a woman?" Finn didn't consider himself particularly progressive, but even he thought that was ridiculous.

"Dad believed that once she got married, she'd end up having children of her own and give up medicine. No amount of talking could persuade him otherwise."

"That's a shame."

"It is, especially because Miriam never married. Never had kids. She's been devoted to her work and has a thriving practice of her own, much bigger than our dad's ever was. She would've been a real asset."

"His loss," Finn said.

Dr. Davis looked at him sideways. "Same goes for the Beachcomber. It's okay to be miffed, son. It's how you handle yourself in the wake of it that offers a glimpse of your true character."

Finn nodded. He liked Dr. Davis, which was one of the main reasons he didn't mind the doctor's failure to choose a property.

"Ready to head back?" Finn asked.

They retrieved their shoes and socks and returned to the patio of the prospective house.

"It's a fantastic property. Marcie would absolutely love it," Dr. Davis said.

Finn sensed a 'but' coming. He remained silent, giving his client a chance to get to it without prompting.

"She'd be out here every morning with her beach chair and a book. Probably text me to bring her a cup of coffee."

Okay, so he was going to take the scenic route.

"But…" And there it was. "…I'm not sure this is the right place for me."

"Do you mean the house or the Hamptons in general?" *Please don't say the Hamptons in general.*

Dr. Davis took his sweet time answering. "There are two kinds of people, Finn. Those who want the ocean on their doorstep and those who want the bay."

Finn wasn't so sure about that. He liked both, not that he could afford either one. A waterfront house in the Hamptons wasn't within his means…yet. He was only forty-two. There was still time.

"I'm a bay man, Finn. I like the calmness of the water. I like to kayak for an hour and then come home for something to eat. I like to fish off the dock."

Finn wondered why this speech didn't happen last summer. It would've saved them both time. He put on his professional mask, though. No point in letting the client know his disgruntled thoughts. He'd complain to Jessica over dinner later.

Finn smiled and clapped Dr. Davis on the shoulder. "Then let's go see a house on the bay."

CHAPTER SEVENTEEN

IT WAS rare that Alice found herself the only passenger in a car, in complete control of the radio. She couldn't wait to see her kids, if only for one night. The solitude in her mother's house made her uncomfortable. She longed for Keegan's droll commentary or Amelia's school gossip—anything to distract her from the inner workings of her own mind. She thought about Ryan more than she cared to admit, although she was sure it was more to do with the Beachcomber than anything else. She even dreamed about him a couple times and chalked them up to stress dreams. In her mind, Ryan represented the winery. That was all there was to it.

"Mom's here!" She heard Amelia's voice before she even opened the apartment door.

Amelia threw her arms around her mother's waist and Alice staggered to the side to keep from tipping over. Keegan sat on the sofa, his eyes pinned on the phone screen.

"You're staying, right?" Amelia's face peered up at her, so hopeful that Alice hated to tell her the truth.

"Until tomorrow."

Ruthie swatted her away. "Let your mother go. You're not a parasite."

Keegan glanced up from his phone. "You sure about that?"

"I'm starving," Alice said, dropping her bag onto the floor.

"How about a sandwich? I can manage that now I've ordered from the store. Your cupboard was bare. It was like living in a nursery rhyme."

Alice brushed past her to get to the kitchen. "Don't exaggerate."

Her mother followed her into the kitchen. "You sit down and I'll make it."

"That's okay. I'm more than capable of making my own sandwich." She opened the drawer in the refrigerator and pulled out turkey, cheese, tomato, a jar of mayo, and multi-grain bread.

"How was the drive?" her mother asked.

"Uneventful."

"That's what you want."

Alice nodded as she slathered mayo on one side of the bread.

"Your children are miserable here, by the way. Thought you should know."

Alice jerked to attention. "Why would you say such a thing? That's not true and you know it."

Ruthie crossed her arms. "Yes, it is. They looked happier at the memorial service than they do here in their unnatural habitat."

"You're projecting, Mom." Alice turned back to the tomato but her hand was too shaky to wield the knife. She added the turkey and cheese and left it at that.

"Am I? You don't seem to be living your best life here either. Don't you want to be happy?"

Alice cut a glance at her. "I've been here less than five minutes. Can I eat in peace?"

Her mother motioned to the table. "Be my guest. Are we still going to the museum this afternoon?"

"Yes, I'll get changed after I eat. Hey, kids," Alice called. "Come in here and keep me company while I eat. I want to hear all the news."

Ruthie retreated to the bedroom to freshen up while her daughter decompressed in the kitchen. She gazed out the window at the people hustling on the sidewalk below. A middle-aged woman walked alone amidst the crowd, her black knit hat pulled down around her ears and her eyes downcast. Ruthie was immediately reminded of a story she'd read years ago about a woman who lost her parents, husband, and two children in the Boxing Day tsunami. They were vacationing in Bali when disaster struck and the devastated woman had gone to live in anonymity in New York City. Ruthie thought of her often, which was strange, she realized, given that the woman was a total stranger. She marveled at the strength of a woman like that, one who continued to rise out of bed, day after day, and rebuild her life into some semblance of normal. Ruthie's divorce and subsequent heartbreak was nothing compared to the loss this stranger had endured. Even Greg's death, as devastating as it was, didn't quite reach the level of tragedy that occurred in Bali.

She spotted an elderly woman hobbling along the sidewalk with a cane, supported by another woman. Her thoughts turned instinctively to Aunt Jean. Ruthie would've been that other woman—the support system—had Aunt Jean not shunned her. It had hit Ruthie hard, especially after being shunned by her own parents. Aunt Jean had become a surrogate mother to her, and Ruthie had embraced the relationship with both arms.

It was the affair that destroyed their close bond. Aunt Jean discovered Ruthie's secret during the summer of Carl's third visit. She'd stopped by unannounced to invite Ruthie to a function at the Beachcomber. Ruthie didn't even remember what the function was now, not that it mattered. She'd tried to explain Carl's presence, a difficult task given the early hour and the fact that they both wore pajamas. Aunt Jean remembered Carl and his family from their initial visit. They'd visited the Beachcomber that week with Ruthie and her kids, and Aunt Jean had let the children run wild in the vineyard.

After Carl's departure, Ruthie had tried to talk to the older woman and explain their situation. That Carl and Laurie had married young and grew apart. That Carl's own father had abandoned his family when Carl was a boy and he refused to continue the cycle. Ruthie even confessed her undying love for Carl, but Aunt Jean wasn't interested. Ruthie's behavior was sinful and abhorrent and Aunt Jean wanted nothing to do with her.

Ruthie's absence from Aunt Jean's will had brought it all back. It wasn't that she wanted anything of monetary value. She only wanted acknowledgement, that she had meant something to Aunt Jean. That she would be silently condemned in death the way she had been during Aunt Jean's life should have come as no surprise, and yet it had been painfully shocking all the same.

There wasn't a day that went by without thoughts of Carl. Ruthie spoke to him, too, sometimes, the way some people spoke to God or the universe. She would tell him about her day or complain about a problem. She'd trusted Carl implicitly. When she'd said this to Aunt Jean, the older woman had laughed bitterly. *How can you trust a married man who would cheat on his wife?*

Yet she had. During their annual visits, she shared all her

innermost thoughts with him. She exposed her flaws and still he returned the following year. The first year that he failed to show up, Ruthie thought his flight had been delayed. As the hours passed, she worried there was an issue with one of his sons. She wasn't sure how she'd survived that week without him. She'd taken time off work and had nothing to do except weep in the house. She didn't dare call, as much as she wanted to. It was a line she didn't allow herself to cross. If his wife answered, Ruthie would have to explain herself, which was impossible to do without destroying other relationships. Never mind that she'd lost Aunt Jean. It was the price she paid for Carl's love and she'd pay it again. Whatever the cost to her, it was worth it.

"Are you ready, Mom?" Alice asked, interrupting her thoughts.

Ruthie turned to look at her daughter. Her age was finally beginning to show, Ruthie thought. Small wrinkles around the mouth and one crease across the brow, a faint line that seemed to grow deeper each day following Greg's diagnosis.

"Is that what you're wearing?" Ruthie asked. Instantly, she wished she could snatch back the words. It was a reflex, but truthfully, Alice's outfit was fine. In fact, Ruthie thought she looked better than she had in years; something about her seemed...lighter.

"Is that what you're wearing?" Alice shot back. "This is Manhattan, remember? What you wear in the Hamptons, stays in the Hamptons."

Ruthie smiled. "Touché."

Chelsea sat at the kitchen table and stared at her computer screen with such intensity that the words began to blend together. The piece wasn't ready, which meant she wasn't going to make the deadline. Her hand moved to rest on her phone. She had to text Ed and let him know, but the prospect terrified her almost as much as handing over an imperfect article. Almost.

She heard the front door open and close and her father's voice rang out, "Chelsea?"

"Kitchen," she called back.

Her father ambled into the room. "There you are."

"Hey, Dad. I didn't expect to see you here."

"Brendan borrowed my drill last week and I need it back."

"Doing home improvements?"

"Penny wants to relocate a shelf." He didn't look particularly happy about it.

"I'm sure Brendan or Finn will do it for you, if it can wait until later."

Her father waved a hand. "You kids are all so busy. I don't want to bother anybody."

"You're not bothering anyone, Dad. If you need help, just ask."

"I'm the one who's retired. I have all the time in the world." He continued to hover in the doorway. "You working?"

"Yes. I have a deadline, but I don't think I'm going to finish in time."

Her father pulled out the chair adjacent to her and sat. "What's the problem?"

She rubbed her temples. "I can't put my finger on it, but it isn't right."

Her father frowned. "What's it about?"

"The father and son who operate flights in and out of the Hamptons."

He chuckled. "Well, it's hardly brain surgery, Chels. Just send it."

"I can't," she said, more heatedly than she intended. "It isn't good enough."

"I'm sure it's fine. You always get so caught up in details no one else can see."

Chelsea didn't have the energy to offer a snarky reply. He could be as bad as her mother when it came to unnecessary criticism. Not often, but sometimes.

"*I* know it isn't right and that's what matters," she said.

He drummed his fingers on the table. "Do you remember that essay contest you were so desperate to enter?"

Chelsea clenched her hands. She was tired of reliving this story, but they never let her forget. They trotted it out as proof of her alleged personality flaw at every opportunity.

"We postponed a family vacation by a whole day so you could revise it one more time before you submitted it."

"I know, Dad. You don't have to make me feel guilty after all these years." She'd made them wait and then froze when it came time to submit the essay. She hadn't been happy with it and decided to scrap the whole thing. They lost a day of vacation for nothing. Isabel and Freddie had sulked and even Penny had seemed irritated, which wasn't typical.

Her father covered her hand with his. "I'm just reminding you that life's short and sometimes you need to get over yourself and say screw it."

Chelsea wanted to ask whether that was his mindset when he decided to get a divorce, but she bit her tongue. She didn't want to pick a fight. Her dad was trying to offer wise counsel and she knew he made a good point. She just wasn't in the mood to hear it.

"The drill is in the garage," she said. "The middle of the second shelf." She only knew because she'd spotted it yesterday when she was out there hunting for the black garbage bags they used for the garden waste. They'd used the last white bag and she forgot to put them on the list so she needed an alternative until she could get to the store.

"I haven't had a chance to talk to you one-on-one," her father said.

"About your angina?"

He blew a raspberry. "Nothing more to say. It is what it is. I'm following the doctor's orders. I was thinking more about the Beachcomber."

She glanced up at him. "What about it?"

He smiled. "I worried your mother might have a stroke when Jeffrey told us about the will."

"You know Mom. She takes everything personally." She would've taken an outbreak of smallpox personally if it had happened during her lifetime.

"Were you disappointed that Aunt Jean didn't include you in the will? I could tell Finn was annoyed."

Chelsea laughed. "That doesn't take detective work. I was surprised, but I didn't mind. I wouldn't have left the Beach-comber to me either. I'd only run it into the ground."

"You underestimate yourself, Chelsea. You always have."

Uncomfortable in the spotlight, she shifted topics. "Are you mad at Freddie about losing his job?"

He shook his head. "Freddie's still figuring things out. I'm glad he's helping Alice, though. He needs a focus or he tends to go off the rails, and what better focus than helping out a sister in need?"

"I'm looking forward to the charity event," Chelsea said.

Her father smiled. "So am I, now that I've tasted the food. It's a shame relations got so strained with Aunt Jean. I wish we'd spent more time there as a family."

"I would've felt like a traitor to Mom," Chelsea said. And even if she hadn't at the outset, Ruthie would've made certain to inject guilt into her veins.

"I'm sure your sister feels conflicted about the whole thing, but she's handling it like a champ."

"Shocker," she said, smiling. Alice was the most capable person she knew.

"It's nice having everybody nearby, too. It feels like an extended holiday."

She laughed. "Only to those of you not working or ferrying kids to and fro."

Her father tapped the table. "Send the article, Chels," he urged. "Let your boss decide whether it's good enough."

Chelsea wished she shared her father's laidback approach. "I'll think about it," she lied.

She waited until her father left to send the text to her editor—and then turned off her phone to avoid the inevitable fallout.

CHAPTER EIGHTEEN

The squawking of birds greeted Finn as he and Jessica boarded a boat in Sag Harbor. He loved it when work and leisure combined, especially when that leisure involved an outing on the water.

"Captain Nolan. Looking good, sir." Finn pumped the hand of his longtime friend. Nolan Honeycutt owned Hampton Waves, a boat rental company that included a fleet of thirty boats of various sizes and budgets. Each boat came with a licensed captain. Finn had sent many happy customers Nolan's way over the years without a single complaint. Nolan was only too happy to return the favor by sending clients smitten with the Hamptons to Finn's realty doorstep. A win-win.

"Great to see you both." Nolan leaned down to kiss Jessica's cheek. "I see you're still the most beautiful wife on Long Island."

"And you still have the most beautiful boats," Jessica said. "You know the Sundancer is my dream boat."

"I thought I was your dreamboat," Finn said with mock disappointment. Finn had to admit, though, that even he couldn't compete with thirty-two feet of nautical luxury. Two sunpads, a plush cockpit, a sleek cabin—Finn was in heaven.

Jessica handed Nolan a bottle of bourbon. "Thanks for hosting, captain."

Nolan admired the label. "One of my favorites. Thank you."

"What time are the others arriving?" Finn asked.

"In about fifteen minutes. There are three couples and two of them are seriously considering a second home here."

Finn high-fived his friend. "Now if only we could get a woman aboard for you, we'd have an even number."

Nolan adjusted the collar of his pale blue polo shirt. "I'm good, thanks."

Jessica nudged him. "What happened with that redhead we saw you with on New Year's Eve?"

Nolan seemed to ponder the question, as though he couldn't quite recall his date that night. "She was only in town for the holidays. You know how it is."

Finn did know. The Hamptons could be a challenging place to date when so many people were visitors.

"You need to stop hanging out at work all the time," Jessica chastised him. "You only meet tourists because they're the ones renting the boats."

Nolan spread his arms wide like he was king of the world. "But I love my boats. I'd rather be enjoying myself on the water than hoping to meet someone in a bar. At least if she's already on the boat, then I know we've got that in common."

He waved in greeting and Finn turned to see three couples walking toward the boat. Each one seemed better looking than the next. The tall, lithe blonde looked straight off a Milan runway. Finn's hand instinctively moved to rest on his stomach. He had a slight paunch now, thanks to indulging in cravings over the winter months, but the sight of these couples was sure to give him the kick in the pants he needed to get back to a healthy lifestyle.

"Welcome aboard," Nolan called.

Jessica tugged her husband back to make room for the others. Finn knew he had a tendency to hover and pounce; it was the salesman in him, so he appreciated when his wife reined him in.

"Jessica and Finn Hughes, I'd like you to meet Cindra and Tom, Avery and Mick, and Marley and Ben."

Finn made a mental note of their names as Nolan prepared for departure. Jessica seamlessly stepped into the role of hostess, offering everyone drinks. Finn never ceased to admire his wife's social skills. He was self-aware enough to recognize that he was the more intense one. Finn appealed to people's minds, whereas Jessica appealed to their hearts. It was one of the many reasons they worked so well together, he thought.

Finn quickly established that Mick and Avery were the most serious about viewing potential second homes, with Marley and Ben a close second.

Ben cupped his hands around his mouth. "Hey, Nolan. Where's your Azimut?"

"On an overnight," Nolan said.

"Damn. I was hoping to check it out." Ben turned to his friends. "That's the yacht I was telling you about with the sundeck barbecue."

Avery perked up. "We should do an overnight."

"You'll have to settle for Shelter Island today, I'm afraid," Nolan told her.

Mick tipped back his bottle of beer and drank. "If we buy a house here, then we can do as many overnights there as you want."

Avery rolled her eyes. "Not the same as a yacht."

Finn held back, not wanting to come on too strong. Good

thing he had his wing woman. Jessica would give him a subtle tap on the toe if his friendly nature veered into salesy territory.

"Finn and Jess can help you," Nolan said. "They're local realtors."

Avery gasped and tugged her husband's arm. "Did you hear that, Mick? We have experts onboard." She faced Finn. "My husband and I can't agree..."

"Welcome to married life," Ben quipped, and everyone laughed.

Avery played with a strand of her cornsilk hair. "Mick wants to buy in Montauk, but I think that's too far from everything else."

"Which area do you prefer?" Finn asked.

"Bridgehampton," Mick interjected, before his wife could answer. "Old money. Old people." He sliced a hand through the air. "No thanks."

"What is it about Bridgehampton that appeals to you?" Finn asked. Privately, he agreed with Mick, but his opinion wasn't relevant here.

"She likes the historic homes, but no way am I getting something that needs constant maintenance," Mick said.

Finn and Jessica exchanged brief looks. Finn wasn't sure if it was the beer's influence or if Mick was just a loudmouth jerk who liked to talk on behalf of his wife.

"I'd consider East Hampton, too," Avery said quietly, "but Mick thinks it's too uptight."

"Because it is," Mick said. "I don't want to spend my summers tolerating people I can't stand. I do enough of that in the city."

"Amen to that, brother," Ben said, and sucked down the remainder of his beer from his bottle.

Finn had the distinct impression that Mick was the one

more likely to get his way in their relationship. The leggy blonde seemed to shut down in the face of conflict.

"Have you looked at Amagansett?" Finn asked.

Jessica brightened. "That's a great idea."

Mick and Avery wore matching blank expressions. "Where's that?" Mick asked.

"It's technically a hamlet in East Hampton," Finn said, "but it has more of a laidback community vibe."

"We have a couple listings there if you'd like to see them," Jessica added. "Even if you don't like the houses, that would at least give you more of a feel for the location."

Mick and Avery nodded at each other. "That sounds good," Mick said. "Let's do it."

Finn pulled out his phone. "Great. I'll make the arrangements." Amagansett was a decent compromise. If they could find a house they liked, he thought the location would meet both their needs.

"You should all go to the Beachcomber while you're here," Nolan said. "Finn's family owns it."

"The vineyard?" Marley asked. "We were there last year for a wedding. It was beautiful."

"My sister owns it now," Finn said. He tried to keep any note of tension out of his voice when he spoke.

"I wish we had a vineyard in the family," Ben said.

"Friends with yachts. A vineyard." Mick clapped Finn on the back. "You seem like the right man to know, Finn Hughes."

Nolan laughed. "That's what happens when you live here full-time. You get to know everyone."

"I grew up here," Finn added. "The vineyard used to be a farm. It's been in my family for generations."

"That's so cool," Ben said.

It *was* cool and Finn wanted to be a part of it. He tried not to let his bitterness show. He saw that Jessica had moved to sit on the open sunpad on the bow with Cindra and Tom. Although it was a short trip to Shelter Island, Nolan was taking the scenic route to give them more time on the boat. There'd be no complaints from Finn. He was happy to stay on the boat all day as long as the weather was this unseasonably nice. He credited their visitors with bringing the fair weather. Finn's luck was never that good.

He dropped down next to Tom, who was in the middle of telling Jessica that he couldn't wait for beach weather to arrive and hoped his friends bought a house in time for all of them to enjoy it.

"How about you?" Finn asked Tom. "No desire for a place of your own to escape to?"

"Oh, I'd love it." He nudged his wife's knee with his own. "We both would, but we've committed any extra funds to fertility treatments."

Finn noticed Jessica perk up. "That's understandable. I hear it's expensive," she said.

Finn wondered whether she knew that from her own research. It wasn't a subject they openly discussed, although he knew they should. It was difficult to get the words out, as though saying it out loud was admitting defeat.

"We're fortunate to be able to afford it," Cindra said.

Finn didn't ask about whether they'd considered adoption. He knew from his own experience that it was a deeply personal choice.

"How do you know when to stop...trying?" Jessica asked. "Is there a point where you just say enough already or where the doctors tell you they've tried everything they can?"

Cindra leaned her head on her husband's shoulder. "It might be foolish, but we decided to keep going until we get pregnant or the money runs out."

Finn wasn't sure that bankrupting yourselves for the sake of a baby was a smart move, but he understood the desire.

"I've had five miscarriages, so we know I can get pregnant," Cindra continued.

Finn didn't know how to respond to a declaration like that. He was accustomed to strangers sharing personal information—that happened quite a lot in his profession—but this one seemed to hit too close to home.

"I'm so sorry," Jessica said. "That must be difficult for you."

Finn brought the beer bottle to his lips and drank, relieved his wife knew the right words to say.

"Two minutes to Shelter Island," Nolan called.

Cindra clapped her hands. "Perfect timing. I'm starving."

Tom stretched before helping his wife to her feet. "That breeze is incredible. You two really are lucky to live here."

Finn grinned. "Convince your friends to buy a house and you can be lucky, too."

"Trust me. I'm working on it."

It was only when the couple left the bow that Finn noticed his wife's face had taken on a greenish hue. "Are you feeling okay?" he asked.

"I think I might puke." She clamped her mouth closed.

Finn examined his wife closely. Jessica never got motion sickness on a boat. Could she be pregnant this time? When she ran to the side and vomited into the water, he had to stop himself from cheering.

He handed her a clean napkin and she wiped her mouth. "Do you think you'll be able to eat at the restaurant?"

She nodded. "Nothing too heavy, though."

He didn't miss the tiny smile. "You don't look too unhappy for someone who just puked over the side of a boat."

She clasped both his hands. "What if...?"

Finn shook his head, willing her to be silent. He didn't

want anything to jinx it. If Jessica was pregnant, they'd know soon enough.

"My mother had morning sickness with me," Jessica said.

"Same, and my mom never lets me forget it." He launched into his imitation of Ruthie, giving him shit for something he had no control over in the womb.

"Come on, you two," Nolan said. "You have time to stare into each other's eyes at home."

Finn had been so caught up in the moment, he hadn't noticed they'd docked. He kissed his wife's vomit-stained lips and held her hand as they disembarked.

CHAPTER NINETEEN

ALICE STUDIED the spreadsheets that the accountant had shared with her. All the columns and numbers were straining her eyes. Ryan had offered to go through them with her, but she'd declined. She understood them; she just hated spreadsheets. As far as she was concerned, there was a special place in hell for the creators of Excel.

The door opened and Ryan poked his head inside. "Hey, how busy are you right now on a scale of Googling Why Cats Have Nostrils to Mach 10 With Hair on Fire?"

She tossed her pen onto the desk and leaned against the chair. "I'm considering drowning myself in one of those barrels of wine in the cellar. Why?"

"Don't do that. You might stain your top."

She glanced at her off-white shirt. "Yes, that would be my biggest concern."

"There are some people here for a tasting I'd like you to meet."

She adjusted the hem of her sleeves. "I wasn't planning to mingle with guests."

"You look great. Don't worry about that."

She blew off the compliment. He was only saying she looked great to get her to the tasting room.

"I could use a break," she said.

"Perfect. You can join in the tasting. The Rubens are the only ones here."

"The Rubens?" she queried.

"They're members of our wine club."

Alice vaguely recalled someone telling her about the Beachcomber's wine club that offered discounts and other special benefits to its members. In fact, she was fairly certain there was a column devoted to the wine club on the spreadsheet.

She didn't have a mirror to check her face. She'd have to take it on faith that she didn't have evidence of lunch smeared across her cheek.

She accompanied Ryan to the tasting room where Baz was setting up. An older couple chatted quietly on the other side of the bar. The man was bald with glasses that seemed to balance on the edge of his nose. He wore a shirt and jacket without a tie. The woman's white hair looked like a soft layer of snow. Alice was sure she'd recently seen the woman's dress in the window of Talbot's.

Ryan guided her by the elbow. "Alice, I'd like you to meet Don and Beverly Ruben."

"Great to meet you." Alice shook Don's hand first, trying not to wince from his unnecessarily strong grip. Beverly, on the other hand, offered two fingers in lieu of an entire hand. She was either a germaphobe or a bitch. Time would tell.

"Congratulations on your new ownership," Don said. "You've acquired quite a gem."

"We adored Jean," Beverly added. "A heavy loss for the community."

"I appreciate that," Alice said.

"I understand you lost your husband a few years back," Don said. "Jean mentioned you on occasion."

Alice was taken aback. Aunt Jean had shared details of her personal life with complete strangers?

"Yes, Greg had pancreatic cancer."

"That explains Light Up Your Life," Don said, nodding. "She was very excited about this event. It's a shame she didn't live to see it come to fruition."

"Have you managed to meet anyone?" Beverly asked.

Alice stared at her blankly. "Meet anyone?"

Ryan cleared his throat. "I think she's asking if you have a boyfriend."

"Oh." Alice was no stranger to an attempted setup, but she hadn't expected it from this corner of the world. She gave her trademark answer. "I'm focused on my kids and my career. There'll be time later for more."

Don clasped his wife's hand. "We're going on forty-one years."

"Congratulations," Alice said. She had no way of knowing whether she and Greg would've made it their forty-first anniversary. They seemed like a solid couple, but so did a lot of partnerships that ended in divorce. After the first few dissolutions in her early thirties, Alice ceased to be surprised by anyone's announcement. Cheating, addictions, religious differences, money disputes, and, of course, death. None of it fazed her anymore.

"We come to the Beachcomber to celebrate all the special occasions in our lives," Don said. "It's our favorite place."

"It's our nephew's birthday today, so we've invited him here for a tasting," Beverly added.

Aha. The nephew.

"Well, I hope you all enjoy yourselves," Alice said.

"We'd like it very much if you joined us for the tasting, if you're not too busy," Don said.

Beverly patted her husband's arm. "Of course she's not too busy to join two of Jean's favorite guests."

Ryan suppressed a smile. He clearly had no intention of saving her.

"I will make time," she said. How could she not? Guests like the Rubens were the backbone of this establishment. If she couldn't keep them happy, the rest would follow. "I just need to take care of something in my office, and then I'll be back."

"Should I wait?" Baz asked.

"Not for me," Alice said, and hurried from the room.

Ryan appeared in her office two minutes later, wearing a huge grin that both irritated her and, if she was honest with herself, made her knees a little weak.

"Have you met this nephew?" she demanded. "You have, haven't you?" She squeezed her hand into a fist. "I should fire you for insubordination. He's an absolute troll, isn't he?"

Ryan chuckled. "Don't worry. He only uses his inhaler in between tastings."

Alice closed her eyes. "Why would they want to set me up with their nephew? This is the first time they've met me. *I* could be a horrible troll."

"I think they took one look at you and realized that Jean didn't exaggerate."

Alice hesitated. "Did she really talk about me?"

Ryan's head bobbed. "Yeah. I mean, she talked about all of you, but she seemed especially fond of you."

Alice's chest tightened. Aunt Jean must've been horribly lonely without the rest of the family. She wished her mother hadn't been so difficult. Then maybe tensions would've eased years ago.

"Do you really have something to take care of?" Ryan asked.

"Yes, I'm heading to the cellar to dunk myself in that barrel of wine I previously mentioned."

He held out his hand. "Come on, Alice. I'll be your buffer."

She stared at his hand with distrustful eyes. "Why do I get the distinct impression you're about to throw me to the sharks and laugh gleefully as you swim away?"

"You've been a lawyer too long. I would never do that."

He was right. She was beginning to think she *had* been a lawyer too long.

She walked toward him and gently pushed down his hand. "I don't think we should walk in holding hands. It might keep Stuart away, but we'd also set tongues wagging."

"Good point."

Alice thought she caught a look of disappointment but decided she must've imagined it. Ryan was just being kind, she decided.

As they returned to the tasting room, Duke intercepted them. Ryan was needed in the vineyard.

"I'll catch up with you later and tell you all about it," Alice said through gritted teeth.

Alice tensed when she arrived at the tasting room and saw that the nephew had arrived. He wore a plaid sweater vest and pleated trousers. He was also bald like his uncle, and wore glasses slightly too large for his face that reminded her of a cartoon owl.

Don beamed at her. "Alice, this is our nephew, Stuart."

"Nice to meet you, Stuart."

Stuart didn't smile. His eyes traveled over her like he was assessing a dinosaur bone for display at the museum and found it wanting.

"Alice is a very accomplished woman. She's a lawyer, and now the proud owner of this fine establishment," Don said.

Stuart gave the interior of the tasting room a quick pass.

"Needs some updating. I can recommend someone, if you're interested."

Alice was affronted, but she refused to let it show. "As a matter of fact, my sister is an interior designer and she's going to work with me on a facelift." The lie popped out so easily, Alice managed to shock herself.

Beverly gasped. "Not too many changes, I hope. I have a soft spot for the Beachcomber exactly as it is."

"Nothing too drastic," Alice assured her. "Isabel was here recently and had some great ideas. It seems like the right time to implement them." Isabel *did* make a few offhand comments about improvements, so it wasn't a total fabrication.

Don's gaze flicked to Stuart and back to Alice. "I thought I had a great idea, but I'm starting to reconsider."

"Will Ryan be joining us?" Beverly asked. "I thought he said he would."

"He was needed in the vineyard," Alice said. "Never a dull moment."

"Jean was smart to hire Ryan," Don said. "The second she heard that big winery in the North Fork was interested in him, she pounced." He shook his head in admiration. "She could be cut-throat, even at her age."

Alice let the information sink in. Aunt Jean had hired Ryan as a defensive measure? Did Ryan know that? She doubted it. She couldn't imagine him feeling the same sense of loyalty to the Beachcomber if he'd known Aunt Jean had only been interested in keeping him away from the competition.

"That's business," Beverly said. "Wouldn't you agree, Stuart?"

Stuart was too intent on scrutinizing the wine in his glass to respond.

"Stuart's an accountant," Don said.

Alice feigned interest. "You don't say. Where are you based?"

"Stony Brook."

"I guess you're still using Jean's accountant," Don said. "If you ever find yourself in need of someone, feel free to give Stuart a call."

"I'll bear that in mind." Baz offered her a glass of wine and she accepted it with gratitude. She was going need more than a taste to endure the Rubens.

"I hear you might sell the place," Don said. "Any truth to that?"

"Jean would roll over in her grave, may she rest in peace," Beverly said.

"I'm focused on putting one foot in front of the other at the moment," Alice said. She had no intention of sharing her private thoughts with relative strangers, no matter how frequently they visited the Beachcomber.

"Well, I hope you keep it in the family," Don said. "That's what Jean wanted."

How nice that strangers knew what Jean wanted more than Alice herself. Thanks for that, Aunt Jean.

"I should probably get back to work," Alice said. "As I'm sure you can imagine, there's a lot to learn. It was wonderful to meet you."

Don raised a glass to her. "You, too. We can tell the Beachcomber's in good hands."

Alice darted through the winery and escaped to the back patio. She wandered closer to the vineyard as she sent a text to her kids, reminding them to finish homework and shower before bed. She knew they'd do it, but she felt compelled to do her motherly duty and tell them anyway. Amelia still followed all her rules. Keegan, on the other hand, stayed up later than Alice these days, despite her best efforts to nudge him into good habits.

She tucked away her phone and remained rooted in place, mesmerized by her surroundings. A gentle breeze rippled through the vines and a beautiful sunset greeted her, a sign of better days to come.

Ryan rounded a corner of the vineyard and stopped when he spotted her. "Long day?" he asked.

She kept her gaze pinned on the sunset. "My days have seemed long for years, but not lately."

"Oh? Why's that?"

She turned to look at him. "I think it's because I'm enjoying myself."

He laughed. "It went well with the nephew then? Should I book a date here for the wedding?"

She covered her face with her hands, mortified by the idea. "Bite your tongue." She removed her hands and looked at him. "That kind of illustrates the point, though."

"Which is?"

"I'm sort of stressed and disliked Stuart, but today was still better than my best day at the law firm." She'd been thinking about it, but this was the first she'd said the words out loud.

"You don't enjoy practicing law?"

"Honestly, I hadn't given it much thought before this. I'm a lawyer. It's who I am."

"It's not who you are," Ryan said. "It's what you *do*. Who you are is something else entirely."

She smiled. "You sound like Isabel." The chill in the air finally caught up to her and she hugged herself. "I've been tired, but it's a good tired. A satisfied tired. Do you know what I mean?"

His eyes met hers and she felt a rush of emotions. "I know exactly what you mean."

"Have you felt like that at every place you've worked?" she asked. It seemed unlikely he'd ever leave if that were the case.

"More or less. Nothing lasts forever, though," he said. "Once the challenge has been tackled, I tend to lose interest."

"Does that also explain the absence of a significant other?" Her own question took her by surprise.

Ryan chuckled. "You would think so, wouldn't you? I don't see people as a challenge, only work. I identify where there's room for improvement and then set a course of action to see if I can make it happen."

"And what improvements have you made here so far?"

A wall of silence formed between them and Alice's earlier conversation with the Rubens turned over in her mind. Did Ryan know that Aunt Jean had poached him as a defensive measure and not to implement his ideas?

"Nothing of significance, which, if I'm being honest, has been a bone of contention for quite some time now." He shifted his attention to the sun as it dipped below the horizon. "I guess you could say Jean ended up being my greatest challenge."

"What haven't you done that you'd like to?"

"For starters, I'd like us to use sustainable practices."

"Aunt Jean wasn't a fan of protecting the environment?"

He flashed a regretful smile. "Jean didn't object on principle. She just..." He faltered. "She was set in her ways. If you don't mind me saying so, I think it became more of a prison than a comfort, but she would never have admitted that."

"Stubborn. Resistant to change. Her own worst enemy." Alice gave a crisp nod. "Yep. She was a Hughes through and through."

Ryan chuckled. "She was also extremely charming and highly intelligent. Are those Hughes traits as well?"

"I have to question the highly intelligent part," Alice said. "After all, she chose to leave this place to me."

"I trust she had her reasons. Jean never made an important decision without giving it full consideration. She was a practical woman."

"She'd have to be in order to keep a business like this going all these years."

"Maybe that's why she chose you. You're a lawyer. You must be somewhat practical."

Alice thought he had a point. "Yes, that's true." Still, it seemed cruel to leave it all to Alice, especially when she was no particular favorite of Jean's. If they had enjoyed a close relationship, then maybe Alice could understand the decision.

"If you like a challenge and Jean wasn't letting you tackle anything…" A horrible thought occurred to her. "Oh, no. Please don't tell me you're thinking of leaving, too."

Ryan raked a hand through his hair. "The key word is thinking. In fact, you should know that I interviewed for another job before Jean died. The timing isn't great, I know."

All her positive feelings evaporated. Without Ryan, there was no way she'd be able to keep the Beachcomber going. Not only would she end up selling and upset her family, but there was the added risk of running the business into the ground before they found a buyer.

"I thought you were happy here," she said.

"Yes and no. I love living here, but I've been frustrated on the job front. Jean supposedly hired me for my ideas on how to update the Beachcomber, but once I was here, she seemed afraid to make any changes. Light Up Your Life was a huge deal because it was the first time she was willing to do something new and I think it was only because it was her idea and for charity." He smiled. "Jean was a sucker for a cause."

Alice thought about Aunt Jean's decision to leave her the Beachcomber. Was Alice, too, seen as a 'cause?' Had the decision been viewed as a charitable one? Maybe. She'd never know now. She learned from Greg that the dead don't speak, so you'd better do your darndest to communicate while you're still alive.

"The woman was almost a century old," Alice said. "You can hardly blame her for being set in her ways."

"Maybe not, but I'm nowhere near one hundred years old and I need work that challenges me. I was feeling stifled here."

"How have you lasted this long?" Ryan had been the general manager for what—four or five years now? That seemed a long time to stick around for someone feeling frustrated and stifled.

"Jean was crafty, I'll give her that. Every time I felt close to making a move, she'd offer me a raise or sweeten the pot somehow."

"In that case, it seems to me you're as motivated by money as you are by a challenge."

Ryan shot her an aggrieved look. "You're angry."

Was she? Yes, she supposed she was, although she had no right to be. This all happened before Alice arrived at the scene.

"Why not quit right after she died like Tawny did?"

"For one thing, I didn't have a new job yet; I'd only interviewed. I also felt that I had an obligation to the Beachcomber and that I owed it to Jean to stay longer, at least until the new owner was comfortable."

"You didn't trust me, huh? I don't blame you. I wouldn't have trusted me either."

Ryan met her gaze. "It's more than that."

Alice swallowed so hard, she was sure he heard a gulping sound. "I appreciate your loyalty to the Beachcomber, but if there's an opportunity you want to take, then don't feel... trapped on my account." Her eyes seemed to search his face. "*Is* there an opportunity?"

He let loose a sigh. "They offered me the position earlier today."

"Where?"

"A winery in Argentina. They'd like to attract more international visitors and they liked what I had to say."

"You'd move to South America?"

"It's somewhere I haven't been," he said, by way of explanation.

"Most people take a vacation to see somewhere they've never been. They don't make plans to live and work there. What if you hate it?"

He splayed his hands. "Then I move on to the next challenge."

She frowned. "Does that mean you've decided to take it?"

"Not yet."

Not *yet*.

Alice's pulse raced at the prospect of losing Ryan. "What if I let you implement some of your ideas? Would you stay?"

"I was considering approaching you about it, but you're not even sure you're going to stay the owner. If someone else buys this place, that could take a year, and who knows what their stance will be on changes? If this place is bought by another vineyard, they might have their own person in mind for the job."

He was right. There was so much up in the air. She had no right to expect him to put his life on hold for her sake.

"Then you have to do what you feel is best for you, Ryan," she said.

"They're giving me until the end of the month to give them a decision. In the meantime, they're going to continue interviewing."

She nodded, shoving aside the feelings of loss that clawed at her insides. "Thank you for telling me."

CHAPTER TWENTY

RUTHIE STOOD in the kitchen with Keegan and Amelia, attempting to show them how to cook. She decided to start with baked ziti. It was her go-to dish when a neighbor fell ill or lost a loved one and Ruthie thought it was important for the children to have a recipe like this in their skill set. Once they realized the work that was involved, they might also be less apt to criticize someone else's efforts.

"Make sure the water is boiling before you put the pasta in," Ruthie advised. "And only a pinch of salt. You don't need to end up with high blood pressure like your grandfather."

"You said salt makes everything better," Amelia said in an accusatory tone.

Crap. She did say that, didn't she?

"How do you know he has high blood pressure?" Keegan asked.

Ruthie laughed. "I was married to him, remember?"

Amelia measured the dry pasta in a cup. "Why didn't you want to stay married to him?"

Ruthie retrieved a wooden spoon from the drawer and set it on the counter. "What makes you think it was me?

Your grandfather and I realized we weren't compatible, that's all."

Amelia piped up. "Penny said you were hard to please and that no one could ever make you happy."

Keegan cut her off with a hard look. "We know that's not true, though."

"Well, it's not true for anyone," Ruthie said. "Happiness comes from within."

"Then you were happy with Pop-pop?" Amelia asked.

"Initially, yes," Ruthie said. "But my parents weren't, which put a strain on the relationship from the beginning. They disowned me when I announced my engagement. Did your mom not tell you that?"

"No." Keegan frowned. "They stopped talking to you?"

Ruthie grunted. "The whole kit and caboodle. No communication of any kind. I thought they might come around when your mom was born, but they stuck to their guns. They never met any of my children."

"What was so wrong with Pop-pop?" Amelia's interest was truly piqued now.

Ruthie almost made a 'where-do-I-start' joke, but she decided to answer the question truthfully. "He wasn't Jewish." She still remembered her father's outrage and her mother's quiet fury. Thanks to Sadie and Ira Alpert's behavior, Ruthie was Jewish in name only.

"Since you ended up getting divorced, does that mean they were right?" Amelia asked.

Ruthie retrieved a can of crushed tomatoes from the cupboard and placed it on the counter. "To disown their own child? No, they weren't right to do that."

"But they thought you weren't compatible, and you weren't," Amelia persisted.

Ruthie regarded her granddaughter with a cool look. "Would you think it was okay if your mom never spoke to you again because you did something she disagreed with? Does that sound healthy to you?"

Amelia lowered her lids. "That would be horrible."

Ruthie handed the can opener to Keegan. "It had nothing to do with who Hunton was as a person. They only cared that he wasn't Jewish."

"Is that why we don't celebrate Hanukkah?" Keegan asked. "I have a bunch of friends who celebrate both Christmas and Hanukkah."

Amelia lit up. "Can we do that next year?"

"That's up to your mom," Ruthie said.

"I think it would be cool to celebrate more than one thing," Amelia said. "My friend Athena's mom is Greek Orthodox and they celebrate two Easters."

The children continued chattering about the different religious events their friends celebrated, but Ruthie stopped listening. It had been a long time since she'd thought about her parents. They were long dead and, like Aunt Jean, there'd be no reconciliation. She wasn't even sure they ever learned of her divorce, although word had probably reached them somehow, just as the news of their deaths had reached her.

The more she thought about her parents, the more she felt the urge to clean and scrub. Sighing, she rinsed the empty can and tossed it into the recycling bin. Her parents didn't deserve her mental energy. She'd buried her memories of them the same way they'd buried her existence. There'd be no legacy to pass on and Ruthie was fine with that.

Once the ziti was in the oven, the kids meandered to their respective rooms. Ruthie began to wash the dishes in the sink, her mind fixating on their earlier conversation. It wasn't a surprise that Penny blamed Ruthie for the dissolution of the marriage. Penny was Hunton's wife, and it made sense that she would only parrot his version of events.

Admittedly, Ruthie's independent streak had put as much

of a strain on their relationship as her parents' rejection. It had bothered Hunton that she didn't need his constant presence. In fact, she would feel aggravated when they spent too much time together. He would complain about her need for space, not understanding the relentless pressure of raising three small children and taking care of a house and husband. If Ruthie regretted anything, it was not having a career. She'd resented Hunton for being able to leave the house in the morning and not return until dinnertime. Ruthie had wanted that, too, but she had no college education and small children who needed her. Hunton bore the brunt of her resentment and their arguments escalated to the point where they knew the marriage couldn't be saved. Neither one of them wanted the kids to grow up listening to their parents fight all the time. If they'd resolved their conflicts in a healthy way, maybe they could've stayed together, but there was nothing good about the way they fought. No positive lessons for their young children. Hunton wasn't without his faults, too. His reaction to conflict was the silent treatment. After an argument, she could go days without a word from him. From what she knew, his relationship with Penny was very different. For that, she was glad.

Despite Ruthie's experience with Hunton, she wasn't opposed to a second marriage. She would've married Carl in a heartbeat. A Vegas chapel. The courthouse. The 'how' or 'where' wouldn't have mattered to her, as long as they were together. If only he hadn't been married with young kids. If only his own father hadn't walked out on him. If only...

It took the advent of the internet before Ruthie learned why Carl failed to return that year and each year thereafter. Every year in April, she hoped to see him on her doorstep. Each time someone rang the bell during 'their week,' her heart lurched and she would feel a sense of crushing disappointment when the UPS driver handed her a package or a

Jehovah's Witness attempted to convert her. At one point, she considered hiring a private investigator to check on him, but she worried that he'd cut her off because he made the decision to stay with his wife and needed to focus on rebuilding his marriage. She never quite believed it, though.

Only when Finn showed her the wonders of the internet years later was she able to uncover the sad truth. She'd searched for his name and address and found a newspaper article in The Des Moines Register that reported the tragic death of Carl Andrews in a car accident. He'd been driving to the airport to catch a flight to New York when a semi-trailer crossed the center line and hit him head on. He was survived by his wife and two sons.

Ruthie squeezed the sponge and set it on the side of the sink. If only Carl hadn't died before they had a chance to fully embrace their relationship, then maybe her grandchildren would know the happy person that dwelled somewhere deep inside of her.

None of it mattered anymore. Not her parents. Not Hunton. Not Jean. Ruthie's life was her own and she realized with a tinge of sadness that she'd never felt lonelier.

Finn sat at his desk in the office and glanced over the new listings, praying for one that might win over Dr. Davis. Even though it was early in the season, it was beginning to feel like a repeat of last year. Finn reminded himself that more properties would be coming onto the market and he would be ready to pounce. Dr. Davis's preference was to buy a place now so that he had the entirety of the summer to enjoy it. He'd made it clear he didn't want to rent again and it was Finn's goal to make sure that his client got what he wanted.

The door swung open and Jessica entered with a bag from the pharmacy. "Sorry I took so long. I wasn't expecting it to be so busy. I saw two people we know, so I had to hide in the makeup aisle until they left."

"I've been checking out the new listings. I see a potential one for Mick and Avery, but it's overpriced."

"What else is new?" Jessica walked over to her desk and dumped two pregnancy tests out of the bag.

"You needed two?" he asked.

"One might be defective. Remember that one that didn't work? It seemed smarter to get two now rather than go back to the store."

Finn felt a flare of excitement. "We're still going with Luke for a boy and Leia for a girl, right?"

She nodded. "Unless you want to switch it up and throw Chewbacca into the mix."

"Still saving that for the dog." On their first date, they'd bonded over the original Star Wars trilogy. Finn had been thrilled to meet a beautiful woman who enjoyed the same movies and television shows that he did. He kept a Han Solo bobble head on his desk and she kept a Princess Leia one on hers. The first time he told her he loved her, she'd smirked like Han Solo and said, "I know," and he'd loved her even more for that.

Jessica tore off the packaging. "We probably shouldn't get ahead of ourselves with names."

"How can we be getting ahead of ourselves? We've been trying to get pregnant for years." Finn even had his own secret list of backup names should Luke or Leia have to be discarded for some unforeseen reason. He knew his siblings were unlikely to use either name, so unless a close friend of Jessica's staked a claim first, they were golden.

She crossed the room to kiss him on the lips. "Wish me luck."

"You *own* that pee stick," he said, trying to sound encouraging. "Show it who's boss."

She frowned. "How about just saying 'good luck?'"

As she turned toward the bathroom, he gave her backside a playful smack. "Where's the fun in that?"

He tried to find something to occupy him for the three minutes or so that he had to wait, but it was impossible to focus on anything except what was happening inside the bathroom—definitely not his usual mindset.

His phone bleeped and Jessica's voice shouted through the closed door, "Did you set a timer?"

Finn winced. "Sorry."

"Exercise a little patience, please. It took me more than a minute to pee. I had stage fright."

Finn thought that was only a guy problem, but he could imagine that the pressure might cause her bladder to betray her.

He entertained himself by pretending to fight an invisible enemy with a light saber. Someday his child would be on the other end with a light saber of his or her own. He promised his niece Daphne that he wouldn't inflict pink upon a daughter unless she absolutely loved the color. Daphne was only fourteen but already vigilant about subconscious sexist and misogynist messages that society transmits to both men and women. After a heated debate over the holidays where Finn may or may not have called his niece 'dramatic' and accused her of exaggerating, Finn started seeing all sorts of subtle messages he'd never noticed before. The color of window displays designed to entice tween girls. A news article revealing the pay gap between male and female athletes. Like it or not, Daphne had opened his eyes to things he couldn't see—or had chosen not to. One night after dinner, he confessed to Jessica that he was terrified of having a daughter.

"What if the world starts regressing and we've brought a

little girl into the world who has to put up with that bull-shit?" he'd asked.

Jessica had stroked his arm and given him a reassuring kiss. "Then we'll make sure she's strong like us and we'll teach her to use her voice."

Finn had thought of not only Jessica, but his mother and sisters, too. They were all strong women in their own way. Yes, Finn Hughes felt confident he could produce a female worthy of their line.

The doorknob turned and Finn straightened, forgetting all about his imagined light saber. He glimpsed his wife's face as she emerged from the bathroom and he knew.

Not pregnant.

The window of opportunity was another month smaller.

Finn tried not to let the news rattle him. He opened his arms, determined to be a pillar of support for Jessica. She was tough, and he both loved and admired her for it, but she was still human.

Jessica eased into his arms and leaned her cheek against his. She was only about two inches shorter, so their bodies lined up nicely. It wasn't a particularly important detail, but it was one Finn appreciated. No kinks in the neck from bending. No weird positions necessary in bed. Finn had experienced that with his college girlfriend, Ming. She'd barely scraped past five feet and he'd turned himself into a contortionist to bridge the gap between them. He was sorry when the relationship ended, but he didn't miss twisting into a human pretzel.

"Next time," he said, stroking her hair.

"A February baby would be better anyway," she said. "Too close to Christmas and they lose out."

It was a weak rationale, but one they needed to tell themselves. They both knew they would take Christmas Day itself if that's when their baby was due to be born.

She slipped out of his arms and padded back to her desk. He didn't have to search her face to know she wasn't crying. Jessica rarely cried, especially over this. Finn sometimes wondered whether she was as tough as he assumed or whether she'd simply grown numb to the repeated outcome.

His phone pinged. A text from Dr. Davis, asking for an update. Finn's sigh was deeper than he expected.

No good news yet, he replied.

No good news at all.

CHAPTER TWENTY-ONE

ISABEL DROVE to Finn and Jessica's for dinner, singing along to the radio. Ever since her steamy night with Mason, she'd been in a constant good mood. He was now spending each night with her, except when Asher came to stay. She was pleased with her progress on the guest house, too. Her only regret was that she'd have to return to the city once the project was completed, which meant finding a new place to live. Thankfully, Jackson said she could take her time moving out, proving once again what a good guy he was. Part of her wished it had been enough.

Isabel barely made it through the front door before Jessica assaulted her with gossip.

"Did you hear about Chelsea?" Jessica asked.

"I did." According to Freddie, Chelsea was no longer writing for the magazine, but Isabel didn't know the circumstances. "Freddie did a happy dance, that monster." He wasn't happy that Chelsea got fired, of course. He was just pleased that he wasn't the only member of the Hughes clan to screw up in the last month.

"Dad said her perfectionist tendencies are holding her back again," Finn said, talking Isabel's coat.

"She's forty-six," Jessica said. "If she hasn't gotten over them by now, I'm not sure she ever will."

Isabel stood at the kitchen island and dragged a wheat cracker through pimento cheese. "I don't think that's true. You only stop growing when you're dead."

Jessica pulled a bottle of pinot grigio from the fridge. "Wine?"

"Sure."

"How does Freddie like the Beachcomber?" Finn asked. "I keep meaning to text him, but the day gets away from me."

"He's enjoying it," Isabel said. "He's been mostly dealing with upcoming weddings because Alice and Ryan are handling the charity event."

"It's too bad he's busy tonight," Jessica said.

Isabel nodded. "I know he was bummed to miss out."

Jessica perked up as she poured the wine into stemless glasses. "Is he going out with that sommelier tonight? I over-heard Freddie flirting with him at the tasting."

Isabel's lips formed a pout. "Freddie told me that's a no go. He said he's been his most charming, but he thinks Baz considers him a member of staff and nothing more."

"I don't think Alice and Ryan have that issue," Jessica said. "In fact, I think something's going on between them."

Finn's head swiveled toward his wife. "The general manager? What makes you say that?"

"I'm pretty sure I overheard them flirting, too," Jessica said.

"And you're just mentioning this now?" Finn demanded.

"We've been preoccupied with other matters," Jessica said vaguely.

Isabel sipped her wine. She preferred red to white, but she wasn't one to make a fuss. "I agree with Jess. The way they looked at each other...There was enough energy between them to power the entire winery."

"Alice wouldn't get involved with the Beachcomber manager," Finn scoffed.

"Why not?" Isabel asked. "They're both single adults."

Finn wrinkled his nose in distaste. "She has more important things on her plate."

"I don't know," Isabel said with a shrug. "He's pretty hot." Her nonchalance only seemed to agitate her brother.

"She can't go mixing business with pleasure," he said. "It's a surefire recipe for disaster."

Isabel inclined her head toward Jessica. "Isn't that how you met your wife?"

Finn swallowed the last of his wine and set down the glass with more force than necessary. "It isn't the same. Alice has been entrusted with preserving a family legacy. She's a single mom. She doesn't have time for casual dating."

"I think you're being unfair and pretty sexist." Isabel dragged a wheat cracker through the pimento cheese and crunched it in her mouth.

As Isabel expected, Jessica came to her husband's defense. "He's concerned about the Beachcomber, that's all."

"And what about Alice? Why not be concerned with her well-being?"

"Now you're the one not being fair," Finn said. "You know I care about Alice. I only want what's best for everyone."

"And you've made it clear that you think leaving the Beachcomber to Alice isn't what's best," Isabel said.

Finn inhaled deeply, his nostrils flaring. "It doesn't matter what I think. The Beachcomber wasn't mine to give."

Damn right it wasn't, Isabel thought.

Jessica must've sensed the rising tension because she swiftly changed the subject. "We're sorry about you and Jackson," she said. "We both liked him."

Isabel maintained a neutral expression. If she looked too giddy, they might suspect she'd met someone new and she wasn't ready to have that conversation, not before she knew this was more than a fling.

"I thought you two were headed to the altar, for sure," Finn said.

Isabel drank more of the wine. "*That* would've been a recipe for disaster."

"Why would you say that?" Finn asked. "You seemed to get along well."

"We got along, but we wanted different things in life."

"You mean he didn't want to get married?" Jessica asked. She turned to check the contents of the oven. From the scent in the air, Isabel guessed they'd be having vegetable lasagna.

"Oh, he wanted to get married, have kids, the whole nine yards." She hesitated. Was she ready to talk about this? Her gaze flicked over Finn and Jessica. If anyone would understand, it might be them. "But I recently came to the conclusion that I don't."

Jessica turned back to face her. "You don't what?"

"I don't want kids." There. She'd said the words out loud to her family. Now they were true.

"What made you realize that?" Finn asked. "Was Jackson talking about it?"

She took another sip of wine. "No. I found out I was pregnant."

Jessica stared at her, a wild look in her eye that made Isabel wary. "Pregnant?" Jessica repeated.

Isabel lowered her gaze, unable to handle the intense eye contact. "Yes."

Jessica shot her husband an accusatory look. "Your sister is pregnant."

"I'm not anymore," Isabel said quickly. "I had a miscarriage." She glanced at her brother with a puzzled expression.

Was this a conservative reaction because she was unmarried? Finn and Jessica weren't generally judgmental about this sort of thing, not that Isabel had ever noticed anyway.

"You're only a year younger than me." Jessica seemed to be talking more to herself.

"I'm sorry about the miscarriage," Finn muttered.

"It worked out for the best," Isabel said. "If I hadn't gotten pregnant, I wouldn't have realized I don't actually want children."

Jessica opened her mouth to say something but then seemed to think better of it.

"I guess Jackson was upset," Finn said.

Isabel fidgeted with the stem of her glass. "I don't know. I never told him about the baby."

She'd suffered alone for those few months. The whole experience had been unpleasant and somewhat traumatic, but it had also allowed her to look inward and examine her feelings. If Jackson had been a part of the grieving process, there was a chance she would've let his feelings supplant her own and then she might not have realized her true feelings until it was too late. Of course, the miscarriage had only been the first step toward self-awareness. It was Mason who'd given her the final push she needed. No matter what happened with their relationship, Isabel was grateful to him.

"Is that why you were on the outs at the memorial service?" Jessica asked. "Because you felt guilty that you didn't tell him about the baby?"

"I'm sure that played a role." She couldn't seem to stop her hands from fidgeting. "The thing is, Jackson is sure he wants children. It would've devastated him to know I'd lost his baby." Jackson, she learned during their painful breakup conversation, had pictured them getting married and moving to Connecticut. He wanted the white picket fence and the dog and two kids. He wanted to coach baseball and drink beer with the other dads while Isabel gossiped with the moms and compared stories from the toddler trenches. Isabel didn't want any of that, except possibly the dog.

"I think it's selfish to be able to have kids but not want them," Jessica snapped. Her face was flushed with anger.

Finn placed a hand on his wife's arm. "Jess, she had a miscarriage."

"Good thing, too," Jessica said. "She doesn't deserve a baby."

Isabel grabbed her purse from the counter. "I'm sorry. I think I should go."

"That's probably a good idea," Finn said.

Jessica jerked her head away, but not before Isabel saw the tears that streaked her face. It had been a mistake to confide in them. She'd thought they were the most likely to understand, but there was obviously more going on with them than she realized.

Finn walked his sister to the door and said good night. He watched her disappear into the darkness and continued to stand at the open door, absorbing everything she'd said. Part of him felt guilty for not knowing what his sister had been going through, but how could he? If Isabel wanted to keep her struggles to herself, there wasn't much he could do about it.

Strangled sobs erupted from the other room and he quickly shut the door to keep the noise inside. He spun around and made a beeline for his wife. Finn found her on the sofa awash in tears. He was so unaccustomed to the sight of his wife crying that he briefly hesitated before rushing to her side.

"Can you believe her?" Jessica choked.

Finn knew there was nothing he could say to make his

wife feel better right now, so he let her vent. He listened as she spewed a string of curse words in connection with Isabel and every other woman they knew who'd demonstrated the ability to conceive. He knew deep down she didn't mean any of it. She was angry and lashing out, and Finn was her safe space. He'd apologize to Isabel later. Right now, his wife needed him and that was the only thing that mattered.

Chelsea had all the ingredients for Brendan's grandmother's meatloaf recipe set out on the kitchen island. Her only addition to the time-tested recipe was a mixture of cheddar and parmesan cheese. It was her way of channeling her creativity without reinventing the wheel. Plus, cheese. What's not to like?

The phone vibrated on the countertop and Chelsea glanced at the screen. There was a short list of people for whom she'd answer an actual phone call and Alice was one of them.

Chelsea put her sister on speaker. "Hey. How are you?"

"Hi, I'm sorry to bother you. Do you have a second?"

Chelsea's gaze shifted to the ingredients. "I was about to make a meatloaf for dinner, but it can wait. What's up?"

"Ryan and I have been discussing some of his ideas for the Beachcomber..."

"Ryan, the general manager?"

"Yes, and we..."

"He's a good-looking guy," Chelsea interrupted.

"That's not why I'm calling."

"Maybe it should be."

Alice laughed. "Now you sound like Mom."

Chelsea huffed in mock indignation. "Take that back or I'll never speak to you again."

"I'm calling because we could really use someone with writing experience."

Chelsea turned to lean the small of her back against the counter. "Is this a pity call because I got fired?"

"No, of course not. Selfishly, I'm glad you got fired because it gave me this brilliant idea."

"Are you buttering up your own sister?"

"Does my sister not need buttering?"

Chelsea smiled. "Butter is an essential ingredient in this house. What is it that you need?"

"Remember how you used to write marketing materials for some of the local attractions?"

"Yes." Chelsea's heart began to hammer in her chest. She certainly needed the work, but what if she couldn't give Alice what she wanted? What if the writing wasn't good enough, but Alice felt obligated to use her work and the Beachcomber suffered as a result?

"We need someone to get the word out about Light Up Your Life. Get the local press interested. The website could also use a complete overhaul. The descriptions sound like they were written by a robot."

Chelsea chewed her lower lip. "Are you sure you don't want to hire a professional?"

"What are you talking about? You *are* a professional. Light Up Your Life is obviously the priority. It's coming up fast and we could really use your wordsmithing."

Tendrils of fear uncurled in Chelsea's stomach and spread to her extremities. "That's such an important event."

"Exactly."

She began to pace back and forth in the kitchen. "You sound pretty invested in the Beachcomber's success. Does that mean you've decided not to sell?"

"Not yet, but I still want to do what's best for the business and Ryan has some great ideas. Even if I sell, everything we're doing now would only boost its value."

"I don't want to let you down," Chelsea said quietly.

"When have you ever let me down?"

Chelsea's fingers tightened on the phone.

"Please, Chelsea," Alice said. "I need help and you're my best bet."

Chelsea shoved her fear aside. For once in Alice's life, she was asking for help. How could Chelsea refuse? "Okay, I'll do it."

"You're the best. Thank you so much. Seriously, you've saved me from hours more work that I can't handle. I'll text you the details."

Chelsea set down the phone and drew a deep breath. She could handle this. The deadline was the event itself, so Chelsea wouldn't give herself the chance to turn on her inner critic. She'd simply get to work. Alice wasn't asking for a dissertation on the history of the Beachcomber. She needed help publicizing a charity event that involved good wine and good food and was important to her family. Now that was something Chelsea could do.

Finn took a chance and showed Dr. Davis the house near the Shinnecock Canal with the hundred-foot dock. The doctor might be older and wiser, but there was one thing Finn had learned that the doctor seemed to have forgotten—the most important decisions in life required compromise, a fact that was omnipresent in the real estate business.

The doctor's eyes twinkled as he meandered through the charming house with its rustic decor. Finn could practically sense Dr. Davis picturing himself in each room. Sometimes a client connected with a house and Finn was certain this was one of those times.

They finished their tour of the house and enjoyed a walk along the dock. Dr. Davis raved over every aspect of the property in his own quiet way and seemed sad to leave at the end.

They returned to Finn's office, chatting in the car about summer plans and Finn resisted the urge to rush the doctor along. He'd make a decision when he was good and ready.

Finn headed inside and Dr. Davis excused himself to make an urgent phone call. Finn thought nothing of it. The doctor frequently stopped in the middle of an outing to speak to a patient. Five minutes later, the office door swung open and Dr. Davis appeared.

"I'd like to make an offer," he said.

Finn nearly collapsed on the floor. He never thought the day would come. Of course, the truth was that he liked Dr. Davis and enjoyed spending time with him. On the other hand, Finn's goal was to sell the man a house. His wasn't a friendship service.

"Was it the dock that sold you?" Finn asked.

Dr. Davis shocked him by saying, "No. I've talked it over with Marcie, and we've decided to go with that pretty little number at the beach. The white one with black shutters."

The beach? Finn was confused. "But I saw the way you looked…and all that talk about bay people versus ocean people…"

Dr. Davis rubbed his forehead with his thumb, a gesture that Finn had grown accustomed to during their time together.

"There are also people who want to stay married versus those who are willing to get divorced." He smiled. "My wife has kindly informed me that she wants to keep the windows open at night and listen to the waves."

Finn couldn't argue with that. One of the best sounds in existence. "But she can't do that in a bay house."

"No, she cannot."

Finn had been surprised by clients' decisions before, but this one took the cake. "I thought you really loved the bay house."

"Oh, I did. It's perfect for me, but my life isn't only about me. You're married. You know what that's like. In a marriage, you're only as happy as the least happy spouse."

Finn understood. "Aren't you going to be sad, knowing it's out there and you've chosen somewhere else?"

Dr. Davis looked at him with surprise. "Quite the opposite, Finn. I'm going to rest easier knowing what's possible. And who knows? Maybe I'll meet the owner of a bay house like that one and we'll hit it off. Then I'll get to spend time there, too. Best of both worlds."

"Marcie doesn't want to see the house before you make an offer?" Jessica would skin him alive for that. He and Jessica were a team, and that meant all their important decisions were made together.

"She trusts my judgment. After all these years, she knows I'm going to make the right choice for both of us." He gave a self-deprecating laugh. "Sometimes there's a bit of foot dragging involved on my part, but I always get there in the end."

They discussed the offer and Finn felt confident they'd be able to seal the deal.

"I'll shoot over an email right away," Finn said. "Congratulations, Dr. Davis. You're going to spend the summer here in your own home. I can feel it."

"Marcie and I trust you to make it happen."

Dr. Davis opted to sit outside on a bench, basking in the spring sunshine, while Finn ducked into the office to email the listing agent, Debbie. She replied quickly to say she'd speak to her client and get back to him, and returned with a counter-offer. The negotiations took under an hour, with Finn relaying updates to Dr. Davis on the bench, where he continued to sit with his head tipped back and his eyes closed. Only when a deal was reached did Finn allow himself to relax.

"The timing will be tight," Finn said, "but the closing should happen close enough to the start of summer so you won't miss the best weather."

Dr. Davis nudged his elbow. "You should be proud of yourself, Finn. This wouldn't have happened without your persistence and attention to detail."

Finn slumped beside him on the bench. "It wouldn't have happened without your loyalty and endless patience either."

"I'm only loyal when it's deserved, you know. Never for the sake of it."

"I appreciate that."

"I hope you and Jessica will come by and see us on occasion," Dr. Davis said. "You'd be very welcome."

"Just tell us when and we'll be there."

Finn had never been more in love with his job than he was right now, and not only because it was his biggest deal to date. He'd worked hard and gotten results. It helped that Dr. Davis was a genuinely nice man. He didn't melt down last summer when he failed to find the house of his dreams. He didn't ditch Finn and choose a new realtor this year either. He persisted in his quest, making compromises in order to achieve his goal. Yes, Finn very much wished all his clients were like Dr. Burton Davis.

CHAPTER TWENTY-TWO

RYAN COULDN'T STAND STILL today. He flitted from the cellar to the kitchen to the vineyard, unable to stay put for long. Light Up Your Life was tomorrow night and he was unusually anxious about the event. He knew why, of course. The charity event was the finish line for the Beachcomber's new owner. Every time Alice entered a room, he swiftly departed unless they needed to discuss an event detail. They both had important decisions to make. He spent last night reading about ex-pat life in Argentina and trying to imagine himself there, but every time he closed his eyes, he saw Alice.

"Ryan?"

He snapped back to reality and there she was again—Alice—in the doorway of their shared office. "Hey, is there a problem?"

"No problem. Duke is looking for you. He said he texted you."

Ryan's gaze swept the desk and he located his phone under a stack of papers. "Oops," he said sheepishly.

Alice eyed him closely. "Are you sure you're okay?"

Ryan thought of the winery in Argentina, waiting for an

answer from him, and knew it was now or never. "Do you have a few minutes?"

"Sure." She entered the office and sat in the chair across from him. "You might want to text Duke first, though."

Ryan shot off a quick reply to buy himself time. Duke's problem wasn't urgent, but Ryan knew if he didn't speak to her now, he might not get another chance.

"I know we've been focused on getting through tomorrow night, but I've been thinking about our conversation."

"Which one?" she asked. "I talk to you more than I talk to anyone these days."

He couldn't decide from her tone whether she thought that was a plus or a minus. "The one where I had ideas for the Beachcomber."

She fiddled with her phone. "I see. And you want to talk more about this now?"

His chest was so tight, it felt ready to explode. "I know it might not matter to you, but I'd still like your feedback."

Alice tucked away her phone. "I'm listening. What else would you like to do?"

Without hesitation, he said, "Expand."

She frowned. "In what way? We already use every inch of square space."

"In Southampton, we do." Ryan stared at her, waiting to see if she'd remember. "When you signed the paperwork for this place, do you remember seeing anything about the parcel of land on the North Fork?"

Recognition flashed in her eyes. "Yes, it was originally part of a smaller farm that had been owned by my family."

"That land is prime real estate and it's being wasted."

"What would you like to do with it? It's not like it's adjacent to this property."

"Doesn't need to be," he said. "I'd like to use that land to plant more grapes so we can increase production."

She clasped her hands on her lap, fully alert now. "What did Aunt Jean say about that idea?"

"She had sentimental attachment to the land. She used to ride horses there as a girl and didn't want to spoil her memories." He gave her a pointed look. "But there are no legal restrictions."

She seemed to take the information on board. "That's definitely something to consider."

"There's more," Ryan said. In for a penny, in for a pound. "I'd also like to acquire a small vineyard in Spain. Not right away, of course. We don't want to expand too quickly."

Alice seemed taken aback. "A foreign acquisition?"

"It's not as crazy as it sounds. Trust me. Others have done it with great success."

She laughed. "I bet Aunt Jean had a coronary when you suggested Spain. As far as I remember, she never set foot out of the country."

Ryan wore a wry smile. "I admit, the idea was not well-received."

"But you feel strongly enough about it to raise it again with me?"

He nodded. "I do."

"And you'd stay if you could implement these ideas?"

Now he felt torn. From a business perspective, yes. On the other hand, he wasn't sure if his feelings about the Beachcomber would change if Alice chose to leave. Her departure could sour him on the place and then he'd want to be anywhere else but here, no matter how many challenges he'd been afforded.

"I think it depends on you." His heart pounded as he asked the one question that had been plagued him from the moment he met her. "Have you decided whether to stay or sell?"

"Let's get through tomorrow night," she said vaguely.

Ryan didn't want to get through tomorrow night. He longed to tell her how he felt right now, but he didn't want to say or do anything that might disrupt the event. Light Up My Life was too important. On the other hand, Alice was important to him. What if she left the very next day and never returned? The sale could be handled by others. Alice didn't need to be physically present for any part of the process. She'd probably let Finn handle everything so she could return to the city and continue on with her life—a life that didn't include him. The prospect tore at him. He wanted to stop time in its tracks right now because it meant Alice would remain right here.

"I should go," she said, rising to her feet. "We have a big day tomorrow."

"And I need to see Duke." He joined her at the doorway. "Sleep well."

"I won't, but thanks anyway."

He patted her gently on the shoulder as a gesture of encouragement and reassurance. It was the most he was willing to touch her. Anything more would ignite a fire in his heart that he worried he wouldn't be able to extinguish. He couldn't afford to have feelings right now, not unless those feelings were directly related to his top priority, the Beachcomber.

"For what it's worth, though, I like your ideas," she said.

He watched her walk away, his head buzzing with all the things he wanted to say. He wanted to tell her that she was the reason he was still here—that he'd stay even if she opted not to implement any of his proposed changes—but he was terrified of scaring her straight back to the city. Fear of making someone else fearful—was that a thing?

Duke appeared in the doorway. "Everything good, boss?"

"Yeah, fine."

"Are you sure? You seem a little out of it."

"Just the usual stress before an event," he lied. He could barely focus on anything Duke said. His mind still running through all the possible outcomes tomorrow night.

"I've been looking for you. Did you test the lights or do you need me to do it before I go?"

"Sure, you can go," Ryan said. "Is Baz still here?"

"In the cellar." Duke stared at him for an extended moment before pulling his keys from his pocket. "I'll see you tomorrow."

"Have a good night," Ryan said. He wandered downstairs to check on Henri and Baz before he left. The lights aside, the wine was the star of tomorrow's show.

Henri was alone in the cellar, typing notes onto an iPad.

"Where's Baz?"

"In the tasting room. Not to worry, he is ready."

"Do I look worried?" Ryan asked.

Henri shot him a deadpan look. "Yes."

Ryan plastered on an easygoing smile. "We've done hundreds of events. Why should tomorrow be any different?"

Henri continued to type on the iPad. "Because none of those events involved Alice."

Ryan rubbed his hands over his face. "Am I that obvious?"

"Understanding chemistry is part of my job," Henri said. "And the two of you..." Gingerly, he tapped his screen. "You go together like Syrah and Zinfandel."

"She's going to sell," Ryan said.

Henri pursed his lips. "I'm not so certain. She seems to have...come alive these past few weeks. And for what it's worth, I think she's as taken with the Beachcomber as she is with its manager."

"Are we talking about Alice?" Baz appeared in the cellar,

looking as haggard as the rest of them. They were all going to need a vacation after tomorrow night.

"How did you know?" Ryan asked.

Baz pointed to his eyes. "Because I have these."

Ryan felt like a fool. And here he thought he'd been hiding it well. He should've known better.

Baz crouched down to examine a crate of bottles on the floor. "I think fear is holding you both back. She lost a husband, so her I can understand." Baz cast him a sidelong glance. "Not so sure about your excuse."

"What about you?" Ryan shot back. "I've seen the way you and Freddie look at each other. If Alice sells, Freddie goes, too. Straight back to the city, the both of them. Is that what you want?"

"You make an excellent point," Baz said, "but when I have no control over an outcome, I find it's best to wait and see how it plays out."

Henri plucked a bottle of red from the crate and opened it. "I think we need to test this one for tomorrow, just to be certain."

Ryan grunted softly. "I like the way you think, friend."

Henri poured three glasses and lifted his. "To what shall we toast?"

"To the one constant in life," Ryan said, raising his glass. "To change."

Isabel opened the door to Hughes Realty and stepped inside. She wanted to smooth things over before tonight's event. There was no way she'd risk ruining Alice's hard work with family drama. Thanks to a little reconnaissance, she knew that Finn was out with a client and the assistant was at lunch. That left Jessica alone in the office.

"Hey, there," Isabel said with forced cheer. She held up a bag. "I come bearing tasty gifts."

Jessica glanced up from her computer, but her expression didn't change. "That's sweet of you." She sniffed the air. "Donuts?"

Isabel settled in the chair across from her and set the bag on the desk between them. "I went to Grindstone and got your favorite."

Jessica licked her lips as she opened the bag and peered inside. "You don't have to be nice to me, Isabel. I was horrible and I know it. I've just been too scared to apologize."

"Why scared?" Isabel asked. "It's not like I've been known to hold a grudge."

Jessica offered a wry smile. "No, you're very easygoing. It's one of the reasons I like you so much."

"You didn't seem to like me very much when I came to your house." Isabel opened the bag and distributed two napkins.

"I'm really sorry. Truly. I was the worst version of myself and I've regretted it every minute since then."

Isabel offered the bag to Jessica first. "I'm sorry you and Finn are having trouble. I didn't have a clue you were even trying."

Jessica took a huge bite of her donut and chased it down with a swig of water from her bottle. "It's so hard not to feel like a failure. I don't want everyone to know I'm incapable of a basic human function."

"What does the doctor say?" Isabel asked, biting into her own delicious donut.

"I haven't seen my gynecologist since my annual exam last year, but, when I mentioned I wasn't pregnant yet, she told me not to worry. That it took time for some women."

"So you've just kept trying," Isabel said.

"Month after month and nothing." She sank against the

back of her chair. "And Finn's been great about it. I'm sure it would've driven a wedge between some couples, but I think it's brought us closer together."

Isabel smiled. "A silver lining is good."

Jessica eyed the remainder of her donut. "I've gained five pounds just looking at this, but it's worth it."

"Why not make an appointment with a fertility specialist?" Isabel asked. "I know of two in the city that friends would recommend."

Jessica gobbled down the rest of her donut. "Part of me didn't want to admit defeat."

"You and Finn are so alike in that way." Isabel thought their competitive natures could easily veer into unhealthy territory if they weren't careful.

Jessica swallowed and smiled. "I know. You'd think we'd want to kill each other, but it only seems to bond us."

"What about the other part of you?" Isabel prodded.

Jessica drank more from her water bottle. "The other part of me is afraid. What if the specialist tells us we can't conceive? I know Finn doesn't want to adopt. As long as we don't know for sure, then there's still hope."

"Every month that passes, you move closer to that dreaded advanced maternal age category."

"I still feel so young," Jessica said. "Finn and I are in great shape. We're healthy. We should be able to do this."

Isabel reached for her sister-in-law's hand. "We all need a little help sometimes. Sometimes from a doctor. Sometimes from a friend. There's no shame in it."

Jessica wiped away a stray tear. "I'm so glad you're not angry with me. Thanks for being the bigger person."

Isabel polished off the rest of her donut and wished she'd brought a third. "You're family, Jess. What hurts you, hurts me."

"Only because you're so empathetic. You and Chelsea both suffer from that."

Isabel laughed. "I love that you see it as a character flaw."

"Chelsea mentioned you're seeing someone," Jessica said.

Isabel grew warm at the mention of Mason. "I am. His name is Mason and he's local."

"Are you bringing him to Light Up Your Life?"

"I added his name to the guest list. We have to drive separately because Mason's babysitter can't get there until seven, so Freddie's going to pick me up."

Jessica's eyebrows shot up. "Babysitter?"

"He has a son named Asher. He's seven."

"Does Mason know how you feel about kids?"

"We've only recently started seeing each other. It doesn't seem like new couple material."

"But he has an actual child, Isabel, not a hypothetical one."

"I know, but me not wanting kids of my own doesn't mean there's an issue. I have no problem being a stepmom, just like my mom was."

Jessica half smiled. "Your mom was an awesome stepmom to Finn. He adores her, you know."

"I do know. My mom's great with kids. I love my nieces and nephews, and I'll be great with Asher, but I don't want to have a child of my own. That's all."

Jessica regarded her. "I still think you need to tell Mason."

Isabel knew she was right. She didn't think it would be a deal breaker, but there was a small part of her that worried Mason would see her differently once she told him the truth. That she'd be less of a woman somehow. Inwardly, she sighed.

There was only one way to find out.

CHAPTER TWENTY-THREE

ALICE ARRIVED at the Beachcomber with her stomach in knots. She was going to have to force herself to eat during the event so that she didn't make herself sick. Carrying an overnight bag, she went straight to room 10 to change. She'd done her hair and makeup at her mother's house, but she didn't want to risk creasing her dress in the car so she held off on wearing it until she arrived. It was a red dress that shimmered in the light, nothing like her usual style, but she'd spotted it in a shop window and fell in love.

Alice hadn't slept well. Wrestling with ghosts of the past, present, and future had left her exhausted, but she was determined to make it through the evening with plenty of energy and a smile. Light Up Your Life deserved the best version of herself and she was prepared to give it.

She was relieved that the staff was too busy to pay her much attention. She dared to open the kitchen door to check on Rosalie's progress, but the look on the chef's face told Alice her energy was better spent elsewhere. It left her free to wander the winery and admire the tasteful decorations. Delicate fairy lights had been threaded across the ceiling of the tasting room and around barrels that were scattered throughout the winery. It wasn't dark enough yet, but she couldn't wait until the winery and vineyard were illuminated. The effect would be striking.

Once the guests began to arrive, Alice's tension slowly started to fade. She acted like a fly on the wall, slipping through the crowd and listening to people rave over the menu and the wine. She had to admit, it was gratifying. Freddie found her hiding in a corner, soaking up a conversation between two older men about how the Beachcomber was their favorite winery in New York.

"How are you holding up?" Freddie asked.

She shushed him. "Hold on. I'm absorbing second hand praise." Once the men drifted toward one of the tables, she faced her brother. "Okay, that helped."

He looked critically at her empty hands. "No booze? I'd offer you my glass, but I know you how you feel about rosé."

"I'm good for now, thanks. I need to pace myself." Alice pointed to the nearby barrels. "I think a pack of elves snuck in overnight to set up these indoor lights. They look amazing."

Freddie grinned. "Is that the collective noun for elves? A pack?"

Something in his expression gave her pause. "You did this, didn't you?"

He shrugged, trying to play it cool, but Alice could see he was proud of his handiwork. "I can't take credit for the idea. I was talking to Isabel last night and she suggested using the barrels as design features, so I got here early and used the lights left over from the vineyard. Baz found me the empty barrels in the cellar."

Alice kissed her brother's cheek. "Thank you, Freddie. It's wonderful."

He gave her a playful shove. "That's enough of that."

Alice caught sight of her father across the room. "Dad's here."

"Oh, yeah. I saw him stalking the cheese board with my mom. And Finn and Jessica are in the tasting room with another couple they seem to know."

Alice's gaze swept the winery for familiar faces. "Anyone else?"

"Isabel was on her way ten minutes ago, and I'm sure Chelsea and Brendan will be here soon. If they're not last, I'll eat my imaginary hat."

Freddie declined his sister's invitation to seek out Finn and Jessica in the tasting room. He was trying to steer clear of Baz tonight, if only to stop from making a fool of himself after drinking too much wine. If Baz were interested, Freddie would know by now. There'd been the occasional moment where Freddie thought he detected a spark between them, but those moments passed so quickly that he was certain he'd imagined them. Freddie excelled at wishful thinking.

He noticed a crowd clustered outside to admire the sunset and decided to join them. The rouge red and burnt sienna sky resembled a painting. Freddie inhaled the crisp evening air and silently thanked the universe for this moment.

"Aren't the lights supposed to come on now?" someone asked.

Freddie vaguely recalled his sister say that sunset would be the key moment when the whole vineyard lit up and awed the crowd.

"Hey, Freddie."

He turned toward the sound and recognized one of the

servers doused in shadow except for the orange glow of a cigarette. "Hey, Nora," he said.

She took a long drag and blew the smoke in the opposite direction. "Great event."

He stuffed his hands into his pockets. "Thanks. Seems to be going well." Once the lights actually came on, anyway. It would be hard to explain an event called Light Up Your Life that didn't have any lights.

"A group of us are going out after this," Nora said. "You're welcome to join us. There's room in the car."

"Thanks, but I think I'll be ready to hit the hay by then. I was up early." He hadn't been able to slow his racing mind, so he'd taken a walk outside at sunrise and immediately felt calmer. Of course, then he was wide awake and ready to decorate the winery.

Nora shrugged. "Suit yourself."

He continued back inside the winery where couples had now taken to the makeshift dance floor. He was mildly surprised by his response to Nora's invitation. When did Freddie ever turn down the chance for more of a good time? Maybe if she'd said Baz was going, he would've felt more inclined, but Baz didn't seem to fraternize with the help, and that included Freddie.

He felt a light tap on his shoulder and his mother slid into view. He thought she looked particularly beautiful tonight in a silver dress and dangly earrings. She was a looker, his mom.

"Care to dance, young man?"

Freddie planted a wet kiss on her cheek. "With the most gorgeous woman in the room? How can I resist?"

She rubbed her thumb across his cheek, like she was removing a spot of jam. "You're a good son, you know that?"

He slid an arm around her waist and clasped her other hand in his. "Am I?"

"Of course you are. You're not Alice or Finn. You know I don't expect you to live your life in a straight line." She smiled. "No pun intended."

Freddie was relieved to hear it. Although he was embracing this next uncertain phase of his life, it was nice to know there were no expectations attached to his decision.

He pressed his forehead against hers. "You're the best mom in the world."

"I do my best." She paused. "I think Aunt Jean deserves a little praise. She seems to have accomplished the impossible."

Freddie knew what she meant. They were all here under the Beachcomber's roof, and there was no conflict or drama. They hadn't accomplished that at the memorial service or the wine tasting, but they'd managed it tonight. Freddie felt proud to be a part of it.

"It probably helps that Ruthie isn't here."

Freddie snorted. "And now it all makes sense."

His father loomed over them. "May I cut in?"

Freddie stepped back to make room and laughed when his father took Freddie by the hand instead and twirled him.

"All those years of dance lessons paid off," his father said, still holding Freddie's hand and swaying to the beat.

"You're confusing me with Isabel."

"Don't think we didn't see the two of you practicing together. Your mother said at the time we should let you join the class, but I only laughed. I wasn't as woke then."

Freddie winced. "Please don't say woke, Dad. It sounds wrong when you say it."

His father's face grew solemn. "I'm sorry I wasn't as attentive to your needs."

"Dad, stop. You've been great." Freddie had no qualms about his childhood. At no point did his family reject him or treat him differently. His dad's lens had been narrow once upon a time, but only because of his own limited experiences. He'd willingly widened it once he learned there was more to see.

"Well, I'm glad you had Isabel back then," his father said. "Makes me feel less guilty."

Freddie glanced over his father's shoulder and spotted Isabel by the open doorway with a half-filled glass of wine. He waved to her with the crook of his finger. "She's always been a good sister."

"You're good kids," his father said. "I'm proud of all five of you."

Freddie clapped his father on the back and let his mom take over. Hunton Hughes was as graceful as a hippo and Freddie didn't want his Dolce and Gabbana shoes trampled.

He felt a pang of longing as he watched his parents glide across the floor, fully in sync. He'd never known two people more content with their relationship. His dad still patted his mother's backside when she brushed past him in the kitchen, prompting a playful swat from her, the delight in her eyes evident. He knew from past conversations that not everyone thought the union would last. People thought his father moved on too quickly because he wanted a woman to look after his first three children. They said Penny was too young for him and would tire of an older husband. But 'they' were wrong, as was often the case when outsiders applied their own beliefs and biases to someone else's life. Their lenses, too, had been narrow, and Freddie suspected they'd likely missed out on wonderful opportunities in their own lives as a result.

Freddie danced his way over to Isabel, ignoring the pull of Baz from the tasting room.

"You look lost, sister," he said.

Isabel swilled her wine. "And it seems I've been found."

Freddie bumped her hip with his. "Do you think we should shake things up a bit? Maybe request a song from the last decade?"

"Don't even think about it. Look around. Everyone's having a blast. I'm not willing to rock the boat."

Freddie gave her a wry smile. "Need I remind you that you already have?" He searched the crowd. "That's who we're waiting for, right?"

Isabel drained her glass and placed it on a passing tray. "He should be here any minute."

He reached for her hand and gave it a gentle squeeze. "I'm really happy for you."

Isabel hugged herself. "Thanks. I'm happy for me, too. And terrified." She threw back her head and laughed. "I'm such a mess."

"Everybody's a mess," Freddie said. "Some people just fake it better than others."

Isabel inclined her head toward the dance floor. "That sommelier is very handsome."

Freddie turned to see Baz chatting with Ryan on the edge of the dance floor. The sommelier caught his eye and winked, sending Freddie's heart into a tailspin. Maybe there was hope after all.

"Speaking of handsome..." Freddie pointed to a figure loping across the room.

Isabel's entire demeanor changed at the sight of Mason.

"For what it's worth, I never saw you look that way at Jackson," Freddie said. He liked Jackson, although the end of their relationship came as no surprise. If anyone had bothered to ask Freddie's opinion, he would've told them from the beginning that the two weren't compatible long-term. Because Isabel had seemed content with the relationship, Freddie opted not to meddle. Like his mom always said, "things have a way of working themselves out." Despite his current situation, Freddie chose to believe her.

Isabel's throat went dry and she couldn't stop staring at him. In a tailored suit and a crisp white shirt, Mason Briggs stood out like a beacon amongst a sea of men. Mason caught sight of her and threaded his way through the guests to reach her.

"Mr. Perfect is coming this way. Should I skedaddle?" Freddie asked.

Isabel was too distracted by Mason to register her brother's words. She also failed to notice when he quietly slipped away.

"Stunning is the only word that comes to mind," Mason said, reaching for her hand to kiss it. The touch of his lips on her bare skin was like a bolt of lightning that electrified the rest of her body.

"Thank you," she said. "You look great, too."

A server stopped with a tray of glasses brimming with red wine, but Isabel declined. One glass was enough until she got through this conversation with Mason. If he didn't want to see her anymore, it would break her heart, but better to know now than two years later. Jackson could attest to that.

She stroked his arm. "I'm so glad you're here. Want to take a walk outside? The vineyard should light up soon, now that the sun set."

They walked through the open doors, still holding hands. She couldn't remember ever feeling this excited over holding Jackson's hand and the realization made her feel horrible. What would have happened if she'd married him? She'd been so certain of their relationship, yet here she was, head over heels in love with someone else. Was she fickler than she realized? She never thought so before, but Mason had her questioning everything she thought she knew about her life. About herself.

They wandered through the vineyard, cloaked in darkness. "Your whole family is here, right?" he asked. "I'd like to meet them."

"I would love that," she said, "but first there's something I need to tell you."

Mason's eyes flickered with concern. "Okay, shoot."

"I don't want children," she blurted.

Mason raised his eyebrows. "Right. Didn't see that one coming."

She continued speaking at a rapid pace. "I know it's early days to mention it, but it seems like the kind of thing you'd want to know. It might be a red flag."

His mouth eased into a half smile. "A red flag?"

"You'd be starting a relationship with a woman who doesn't want kids when you already have one. And you might want more." Her face grew flushed. "I'm not saying I don't want to spend time with Asher, or that I think he'll be in the way or anything monstrous like that. I'm just talking about me—that *I* don't want to bring a child into the world." Inwardly, she cringed. She was explaining this very badly. So badly, in fact, that she wouldn't blame him at all if he walked away right now.

Mason hooked his thumb under her chin. "Isabel Hughes, are you trying to get out of a relationship with me?"

She shook her head adamantly. Definitely not. She wanted this more than she'd ever wanted anything in her life.

"I just thought you should know, so you have all the information at the outset. I don't want to waste your time, or mine."

He gazed at her with such affection, she thought her heart would burst into pieces. "Nobody ever has all the information at the outset—that's not how relationships work—but I appreciate your candor all the same."

Her throat thickened. "Then it's not a deal breaker for you?"

"As long as your ideal version of a stepmother isn't from Snow White, then no."

Isabel threaded her fingers through his and kissed his hand. "Of course not. Asher's a piece of you, Mason and I love that."

"Good, then we're on the same page." He hesitated. "It might be a little challenging with you in the city and me in the Hamptons, but I think we can make it work."

She bit back a smile. "Here's the thing—I've decided not to go back to the city. I'm going to find a place to live here and see if I can pick up some new clients once I've finished with the guest house."

His relief was palpable. "You're sure? I don't want you to give up anything for my sake. You'd only resent me later."

"I'm sure," she said. "If I can't get a foothold here, I can always go back to the city."

"I like your attitude," he said. "Cautious but willing to take the risk."

She gazed into his eyes. "My gut says go for it."

Mason inched closer to her. "What do you know? So does mine." He leaned down and brushed his lips against hers.

Isabel melted against him, not caring whether anyone saw them. She was in love and she wanted the whole world to know it.

Steeped in darkness, Alice took advantage of the moment and admired the brilliant night sky. The full moon glowed, and the sky was so dark that every single star seemed visible tonight. The lights would switch on soon. In the meantime, the guests could gawk at the heavens.

Ryan's voice drifted over to her, soft and soothing. "The discovery of wine is of greater moment than the discovery of a constellation. The universe is too full of stars."

Alice twisted to look at him. "What drunk guy said that?"

A smile tugged at the corner of his mouth. "Benjamin Franklin, allegedly."

"Sounds more like Jefferson," she said. "Wasn't he the one with tens of thousands of wine bottles in his personal collection?"

Ryan laughed and joined her at the edge of the vineyard. "You say that like it's a bad thing. Are you disparaging one of our most venerated Founding Fathers?"

"I think Ben Franklin's deserving of his own musical." Alice wrapped her arms around herself to stave off the mild chill in the air. She should've worn an extra layer, but she'd wanted to show off her dress. Vanity over comfort. Good heavens, she was turning into her mother. A couple of caustic remarks and the transformation would be complete.

"Shouldn't the lights have switched on by now?" Alice asked. She'd been trying to keep her nerves at bay, but now that Ryan was here, she felt compelled to ask.

"I thought maybe I remembered the time wrong," Ryan admitted.

"Sunset," Alice said. "And that's come and gone."

Duke appeared behind them. "I hate to be the bearer of bad news, but the lights aren't working."

So much for keeping her nerves at bay.

"Are you sure?" Ryan asked.

Duke gestured helplessly to the vineyard. "Do you see any functioning lights?"

Terrific. There could be no Light Up Your Life event without actual lights. Alice struggled to keep her composure.

Glitches were bound to happen at a big event. It was how you reacted to them that mattered.

"Okay, we've got this," she said, with an air of confidence she didn't feel. *Fake it till you make it*, that had been her motto ever since Greg's cancer invaded their lives. But she didn't want to fake anything, not anymore. She wanted her life to be real and authentic.

"I let myself get too caught up in the event," Ryan admitted. "I should've paid closer attention."

Alice clapped her hands together. "Okay. Here's the deal. There's no program with specific times, so the guests don't need to know there's a delay. In fact, it will make the moment even more special when the lights do come on." Because they would. They had to.

Duke glanced warily at the lights currently drenched in shadow. "I hope it's not like Christmas, where we have to find the one bulb that doesn't work."

Ryan shifted into manager mode. "Duke, you check the breakers. Alice and I will check the fuses."

"In the dark?" Alice asked.

He held up his phone and clicked on the flashlight app. "Technology for the win."

Duke disappeared and Alice turned on the flashlight app of her phone and followed Ryan into the vineyard. "If it's a fuse, wouldn't it only be one section that's out?" she asked.

"Not sure, but I feel like we need to check every possibility."

As daunting as the prospect was, Ryan was right. "I think we need more than the two of us if we intend to check every fuse before the end of the night," she said.

"I don't want to pull the servers away. They'll keep the guests occupied with food and drink, and hopefully that will distract from the lack of light."

He made a good point. "What about Freddie and Isabel? They can help. Chelsea and Finn, too."

"If they're willing, great," Ryan said.

Alice sent a group text as fast as her fingers could type. She'd never be able to type with her thumbs the way her kids did, but so what?

Finn was the first to respond—because of course he was. *Where do we start?*

Alice's heart swelled as the rest of her siblings replied with offers of assistance.

Minutes later, her family swarmed the vineyard, shooting off into separate directions to divide and conquer. Alice hurried along the path, annoyed that she chose tonight to wear heels. They kept sticking in the damp ground and she worried about losing a shoe in the dark. It was fine for Cinderella, but Alice didn't have time to hobble awkwardly around the vineyard.

She received a text each time someone checked a fuse. Finn's messages sounded like a military operation—*northeast quadrant checked*. Chelsea's messages were vague—*nothing to report*. Isabel's texts were more concerned with her surroundings—*you can really smell the salt in the air tonight!* And Freddie...Well, Freddie didn't check in until someone nudged him. Alice wouldn't have been surprised to learn he'd been lured by the call of the sirens and wandered to the beach.

Her fingers began to feel numb and she had a hard time fiddling with the fuses, as well as angling the phone so she could see what she was doing. The little trapdoors were hard to open. She focused on her breathing as she worked. The event could still be salvaged even without the lights. She'd think of something. As though reading her mind, Finn sent a text with a backup plan involving candles that sounded like a fire hazard. They didn't need firemen bursting onto the scene. She'd leave that to her mother's house.

Before Alice could reply, Isabel chimed in and suggested battery-operated candles. She knew where she could source a large number of them on short notice. Alice felt overwhelmed with gratitude. Whatever happened, the event would be okay. *She* would be okay.

She typed a response to Isabel. Just as she was about to hit send, white lights flashed right in front of her eyes, nearly blinding her. The sound of applause rippled through the air. Her eyesight adjusted and a relieved breath seeped from her mouth.

"Let there be light," someone yelled.

Alice nearly melted into a puddle. As calm as she'd appeared on the outside, her insides had been screaming for mercy. She didn't know whether it was the result of Duke testing the breakers or one of her siblings finding the faulty fuse, nor did she care. The problem was solved—hallelujah!

Her eyes widened at the sight of transformation. She had no idea the vineyard could look so...magical. White lights illuminated the entire vineyard and Alice thought it was one of the most breathtaking things she'd ever seen.

She didn't want to leave this place. She didn't want to sell the Beachcomber.

The realization hit her swiftly and with such force, she nearly lost her footing. It occurred to her that she was more like Aunt Jean than she'd been willing to admit. She'd thought Aunt Jean's resistance to change was such a shame, yet Alice realized she'd been living a similar life. Ever since Greg's death, she'd fought to preserve their way of life, but that life no longer existed and no amount of preservation or list-making would change that fact. Greg was gone. Alice and the children were here and they had to surrender to their circumstances and adapt. Like Aunt Jean, Alice had been stubborn and resistant to anything new. She did hate her job. In fact, she hated the whole life she'd constructed for herself. For whatever reason, that life didn't work without Greg.

Alice knew it was time to stop overthinking her decisions and take a leap of faith.

Ryan rounded a corner and saw Alice alone in a secluded section of the vineyard. "What a relief."

"No kidding." She waved a hand toward the closest string of lights. "I don't understand what happened, though. You tested them last night. What could've changed between now and then?"

Ryan winced. "About that...I'm sorry. It was entirely my fault. I...I didn't actually test the lights last night because I forgot." He couldn't bring himself to say why, that he'd been so distracted by his feelings for her that he forgot such an important task.

Alice stared at him in a way he couldn't interpret. Did she know? Did she hate him for ruining such an important event?

"Alice? Are you okay?"

She shook her head. "Yes, I just wasn't expecting you to apologize."

Ryan didn't know what to make of that. "Because you thought it was someone else's fault?"

"No, no. I'm not interested in blaming anyone. I'm not used to getting an apology, that's all."

Ryan learned early on that people appreciated a genuine apology, so he didn't hesitate to give them what they needed when the situation called for it. He'd gotten out of plenty of jams with a heartfelt apology. To deny responsibility seemed like a waste of time and energy.

"I would've mentioned it sooner, but, to be honest, I

forgot that I forgot until now." He laughed at the absurdity of his remark.

"It's all fixed now. No harm done." She pointed upward. "Plus, we were treated to an amazing view of the night sky. Bonus."

Ryan gazed at her in awe. She'd remained calm, come up with a plan, looked on the bright side…He'd never known a woman quite like her.

"I want you to be the first to know I'm not taking the job in Argentina," he said. "I've decided to stay here."

Alice splayed a hand across her chest. "Well, that's a huge relief because I've decided not to sell."

He stared at her, transfixed. "You're staying, too?"

Alice nodded. "My mother's right. The kids and I haven't been happy. It's time for a change." She paused. "Please don't ever repeat the part about my mother."

"Straight into the vault," he said, pretending to turn a key in front of his mouth.

A smile touched her lips as she surveyed the vineyard. "You have no idea how happy I am that you're staying. I think we make a good team, don't you?"

When she turned to look at him, Ryan couldn't take it any longer. He cupped her cheeks in his hands and kissed her fully on the mouth. Her lips were soft and inviting and, for a moment, it was as though they'd stepped out of time.

Alice was keeping the Beachcomber and staying in the Hamptons. He could hardly believe his luck.

Someone cleared their throat and they jumped apart.

"Sorry to interrupt," Finn said.

Her cheeks tinged with pink, Alice looked as flustered as Ryan felt.

"Was it one of your fuses?" she asked.

Finn shook his head. "An overloaded circuit, apparently. Someone named Duke fixed it."

She smoothed the front of her dress, as though Ryan's lips might've somehow wrinkled the crepe fabric.

"Thanks for letting us know," she said.

"Yeah, I probably should've texted." Finn said. "I wanted to make sure you weren't freaking out, which I can see you're not, so I'll get out of your way."

Once Finn disappeared around the corner, she flung her arms around Ryan's neck and kissed him again.

Ryan moved his arms to encircle her waist. "I've been wanting to do this since the moment I met you," he whispered.

She arched a skeptical eyebrow. "The very moment, huh?"

"It was like being struck by lightning," he admitted.

"If you tell me I light up your life, I'm out of here."

Ryan grinned as he leaned his forehead against hers. "You have to admit, it's a beautiful song."

Finn wiped the beads of sweat from his brow as he headed back to the winery. So it was true about Alice and the general manager. He loved Alice, but he lacked the imagination to see her as anything more than his responsible older sister. Sure, she had two kids, which meant she'd been sexually active at some point during her marriage, but he was more inclined to think Keegan and Amelia had appeared on earth in much the same way as baby Jesus.

"Finn, wait up."

He craned his neck to see Alice hurrying to catch up with him. "You don't need to explain," he said. "It's none of my business."

She shook her head. "No, not about that. There's something I want to talk to you about." She drew a breath. "I've been doing a lot of thinking lately and I'd like you to be part of the Beachcomber."

Finn balked. "So does that mean you've decided not to sell?"

"Nope, not selling. I'm quitting my job and moving the kids here full-time."

Finn's face contorted through a series of emotions and he could tell his sister was trying to identify each one as it passed over his features. Shock. Relief. Elation with a touch of annoyance mixed in.

"I can't believe it," he said under his breath.

She squinted at him. "You can't believe it because it's insane or because you're happy?"

"I thought for sure you'd sell." In a rare display of affection, Finn threw his arms around her, nearly toppling them over in the process. "I'm thrilled, Alice. Honestly. It's great news all around." The Beachcomber. More time with his niece and nephew. He was definitely pleased.

"What do you think? Are you interested in joining the family business?"

Finn was still smiling when he said, "No, I don't think I will, but thank you all the same."

She narrowed her eyes. "Is this because you're upset about not inheriting it in the first place?"

"No, although I admit I was somewhat bitter. The thing is, I already have a family business that I love." He gazed at the vineyard behind them. "But I do like knowing this place is here, in your capable hands, and that I can come by whenever I want."

"Of course you can. The Beachcomber is a family business, and you're family, Finn."

"Does that mean Freddie will continue to work here?"

"Yes, and I'm going to ask Chelsea to handle marketing and publicity. She did a great job for this event on short notice and I think she's perfect. I'm also going to ask Isabel to give the place a decorating upgrade. She's always full of good ideas. Do you think she'd be interested?"

"I'm sure she would, now that she plans to live here full-time." He motioned toward the winery. "Have you met her new boyfriend yet? Seems like a nice guy."

Alice craned her neck for a glimpse of the couple. "Not yet, but I'll make it my mission tonight." She smiled at him. "I'm glad you're happy with the way things worked out. I wasn't sure."

He dragged a hand through his hair. "I wasn't either until recently. I'm proud of you, Alice. This whole thing had to be intimidating as hell, but you took it on like a champ."

"It wasn't part of my plan," she said, "but so few things in my life have happened the way I expected. I've learned that the best offense *and* defense is being open to change."

Finn regarded her silently for a moment. "Yeah, that makes sense." He scanned the winery for his wife. "Congrats, sis. You deserve this and so much more." He chuckled to himself. "So all three of you are moving back to the Hamptons. What would Aunt Jean say?"

"I think she'd say that everything went according to plan," Alice said with a smile.

Finn wished he could say the same. He'd pictured himself with at least two kids by now, but he was done feeling sorry for himself. His sister was right. It was time to stop expecting things to turn out a certain way and be open to a new path.

Armed with this new mindset, he went in search of his wife and found her at the cheese table, deliberating between two types of cheese that Finn couldn't name. "Go crazy and take them both," he said.

Jessica cut a glance at him. "Says the man who sheds calories just from thinking about exercise."

He told her about Alice's offer and watched her eyes register surprise.

"What did you say?"

"I said no."

She nodded. "I guess that's the end of it then."

He snaked an arm around her waist. "There's something else."

"Cheese?" She popped a piece into his mouth.

As he chewed and swallowed the nutty cheese, he tugged her to a quiet corner of the room. "There's something I want to say before I lose the nerve."

She eyed him skeptically. "How many glasses of wine have you had?"

He smiled. "I'm sober, Jess. That's why I want to say this now. I'd like us to see a fertility specialist."

Jessica did something he was wholly unprepared for—she burst into tears.

"Oh no. I'm sorry. I didn't mean to upset you." He hugged her close and felt the powerful beating of her heart.

"I'm not upset." She pulled back and wiped away the tears with the back of her hand. "I'm ecstatic. I've been wanting to suggest it forever, but I was afraid of how you'd react."

Finn felt ashamed. He wanted his wife to feel comfortable saying anything to him, but his pride had kept her quiet about her deepest desire.

"I'm sorry I've been such an idiot," he said.

She smiled at him, her eyes still misty. "I'm as much to blame. I've been researching specialists, but I didn't want to go behind your back, and I didn't have the nerve to bring it up either." She gave a helpless shrug. "We both suck."

"This is an equal partnership, Jess. I like that we're a team." He brushed his lips against hers. "I've let you down and I'm so sorry."

"We're in this life together. Whether we have kids or not. Whether our business succeeds or not. We have each other."

He inclined his head. "Why do I feel like you're about to break into a Bon Jovi song?"

Jessica laughed and the sound was music to his ears. When was the last time he'd made her laugh? He couldn't remember.

"I love you," he said.

Her smile was sexy and flirtatious. It was the smile that had reeled him in the day they met.

"I know," she said.

CHAPTER TWENTY-FOUR

RUTHIE WAS RELIEVED to be back in her own home. Even better was the shocking news that Alice and her kids would be moving to the Hamptons at the end of the school year. As much as she wanted to gloat, she knew her pestering had nothing to do with Alice's decision. Something about her time at the Beachcomber had changed her, and not a moment too soon as far as Ruthie was concerned.

A padded envelope had arrived from Sturgeon & Associates while she was in the city and Alice had left it on the kitchen counter for her. For a fleeting moment, Ruthie wondered whether there'd been a mistake with the will. Maybe Aunt Jean had written several drafts over the years and a later version had been located.

She felt a stab of guilt for allowing the thought. Was that what she wanted—for her daughter to experience loss all over again now that she finally seemed settled? Alice seemed more upbeat than she had in years and Ruthie had no doubt it was the change in scenery. She'd pestered her oldest child for years to come back to the Hamptons, to raise her kids close to family now that Greg was gone, but Alice had seemed set in her ways. Forty-eight going on ninety-eight. Aunt Jean used to call Alice an old soul, but Ruthie suspected it was because the older woman recognized some of herself in Alice.

As Ruthie continued to stare at the envelope, she felt her stomach clenching. Did her selfishness—her deep desire to be loved and acknowledged—truly rise to the level of wanting to supplant her own daughter? No, it did not. Besides, Ruthie didn't want the Beachcomber. She only wanted to be acknowledged by Aunt Jean, to know that the older woman still considered her family, despite their estrangement.

Blowing out a breath, Ruthie tore open the envelope with shaking hands. With her luck, it would be Aunt Jean's unpaid legal bill, adding insult to injury.

Quickly, she scanned the contents of the letter.

Dear Mrs. Hughes:

My assistant located the enclosed item in a mislabeled file box. On it was a Post-It note with your name, written in my client's hand-writing. As no instructions were given for this particular item, I decided the best course of action was to send it to you, as it seems clear that Jean intended for you to have it.

My deepest condolences and apologies for misplacing the item in the first place.

Kindest regards,
Jeffrey Sturgeon, Esq.

. . .

Ruthie set down the letter, perplexed. What was the item? What could be so small that it fit in this padded envelope?

She turned the envelope upside down and watched as a delicate object slid onto the counter. Ruthie gaped at the item, unable to believe her eyes.

In front of her was the moon shell she and Carl had found on the beach more than twenty years ago. The one she'd kept in pride of place on the mantlepiece until its mysterious disappearance.

She ran the pad of her finger across its smooth exterior, remembering how Carl had touched the shell in much the same way. He'd been transfixed by its appearance just as she'd been transfixed by his.

Aunt Jean must have figured out its significance to her and taken the shell as punishment the last time she came to the house. It wasn't impossible. Ruthie wasn't known to be sentimental. She didn't hang childhood artwork on the fridge or adorn the walls with annual school photos. Yet she'd kept a single shell on the mantlepiece, a red flag to someone like Aunt Jean who knew her secret. And Aunt Jean's final visit to the house had been unpleasant, to say the least. She'd spotted Ruthie and Carl at a restaurant in town and was incensed that Ruthie was still involved with him, despite her disapproval. She'd arrived at the house a few days after Carl left town to give Ruthie a piece of her mind. She told Ruthie she was foolish for wasting her life, waiting on a man who would never be hers. Had Ruthie marched her to the door? She couldn't remember now. At some point, though, Aunt Jean had managed to swipe the precious shell from the mantlepiece before her departure.

Ruthie wanted to be outraged by Aunt Jean's thievery, but she felt only gratitude. After all, the older woman could've disposed of the shell. Tossed it back onto a beach or given it to a small child. She also could've gossiped and told everyone why she cut Ruthie out of her life. But Aunt Jean had done none of those things.

Ruthie curled her fingers around the shell and closed her eyes. To think after all these years that Aunt Jean would be the one to return a piece of Carl to her was unimaginable, yet here it was.

Some people don't want to be happy.

The truth was that Ruthie desperately wanted to be happy, but the news of Carl's death had settled in her bones and infected the marrow. She knew then that she'd live the rest of her life alone because the idea of being with a man who wasn't Carl was repugnant to her. But just because she wasn't interested in a romantic partner didn't mean she had to be lonely. That part was a choice. What was it that she'd told her grandkids? *Happiness comes from within.*

Ruthie brought the shell to her lips and kissed it. Soon, she would have all her children and grandchildren in the Hamptons full-time. She would be welcome again at the Beachcomber. Maybe she'd host an engagement party there, if Alice ever chose to remarry. It felt good to imagine the future in a positive light. She didn't realize how badly she needed that until now.

Tears splashed on her cheeks, but she didn't bother to wipe them away. Ruthie held the shell against her chest, close to her beating heart. Her family was here and, to the extent possible, she'd been reunited with the love of her life. A sense of calm washed over her, and gratitude rinsed away all remaining traces of bitterness and resentment. No matter how the rest of her life unfolded, Ruthie would never be lonely again.

.   .   .

Alice drove along the highway with the sunroof open, humming under her breath. Her hair would be a tangled mess by the time they arrived, but she didn't care.

"Will you tell us now where we're going?" Amelia asked from the backseat.

"You'll find out when we get there," Alice said.

"We're headed east," Keegan said. "Are we going to a marina?"

Alice pretended to zip her lips.

"I can't do a boat ride without my sea bands," Amelia said.

"You don't need your sea bands." That was as much as Alice was willing to say.

"How many mints have you had?" Keegan asked.

Amelia glared at her brother. "What's the difference? You're not the one eating them."

"No, but I'm the one who'll end up with barf bits in the back of my hair."

Amelia crossed her arms. "Mints don't make people sick."

"Too much of anything can make you sick," Keegan argued.

"We're almost there," Alice said. "If she's going to be sick, she can do it outside."

"I'm not going to be sick," Amelia insisted.

Alice turned her attention to the road ahead. She was relieved that the weather was now on their side. The sky was overcast when they left her mother's house, and Alice worried there'd be rain on their parade. By the time they reached Montauk, though, the ominous stretch of gray clouds had made a graceful departure, leaving only a slate of blue in its place.

The lighthouse came into view and, with it, Amelia's megawatt smile. Her father's smile.

"Here we are," Alice said.

"I remember this!" Amelia's excitement prompted Keegan to look up from his phone.

"Yeah, this place is cool," he agreed. "Hey, isn't that Uncle Finn?"

Alice smiled. "Good eye."

"That's funny. What's he doing here?" Amelia asked.

Alice parked the car and turned to look at her children. "He's going to show us some houses here, if that's okay with you."

Alice could've driven a tractor truck through Amelia's gobsmacked mouth.

"You mean to live in?" Amelia asked.

Keegan rolled his eyes. "No, to admire from the outside. What do you think?"

"You'll be finished school soon," Alice said. "If I buy a house now, we'll have time to get you situated here before school starts, plus we'll have the summer to enjoy the beach."

Amelia vibrated with excitement. "Yes!"

"What about your job?" Keegan asked. Alice was relieved to note that he didn't sound unhappy, just curious.

"I've decided to keep the Beachcomber," Alice said, "and I'd like to be involved in the day-to-day operations, which means quitting my job and leaving the city. Uncle Freddie, Aunt Chelsea, and Aunt Isabel are going to work there with me."

Amelia and Keegan exchanged surprised glances. "You're all going to work *together*?" Keegan asked.

"And we're going to live here?" Amelia added, equally incredulous.

"That's the plan, but I'm open to objections," Alice said. "For what it's worth, I think Daddy would support my decision."

After an extended moment of silence, Keegan nodded thoughtfully. "Yeah, he would."

Amelia poked her head between the seats. "I support you. I want to move here today!"

Alice waved to Finn, who'd finally spotted them. "I don't know that today is feasible, but let's see what we can do." She turned back to Keegan. "You'll be off to college in two years. If you want to go back to the city then and be closer to your friends, it's not very long to wait."

Keegan glanced out the window at the landscape. "Do you think it'd be okay if I invite my friends to visit us over the summer break?"

"Absolutely." Relief flooded her and Alice opened the door to breathe in the fresh air. Yes, Greg would definitely approve. Although she would've done what was best for her family either way, believing he'd be supportive made her feel better about the decision.

"Hey, there," Finn greeted them. "I've got some great houses lined up for us to see today. Are you ready to find your new home?"

"Yes," the kids said in unison.

Alice felt a rush of excitement. Change was coming and, this time, she was ready for it.

* * *

Thank you for reading. If you enjoyed this book, please sign up for my newsletter http://eepurl.com/clRdh5. You can also check out my website at nevecottrell.com and find me on Facebook https://www.facebook.com/nevecottrell/.

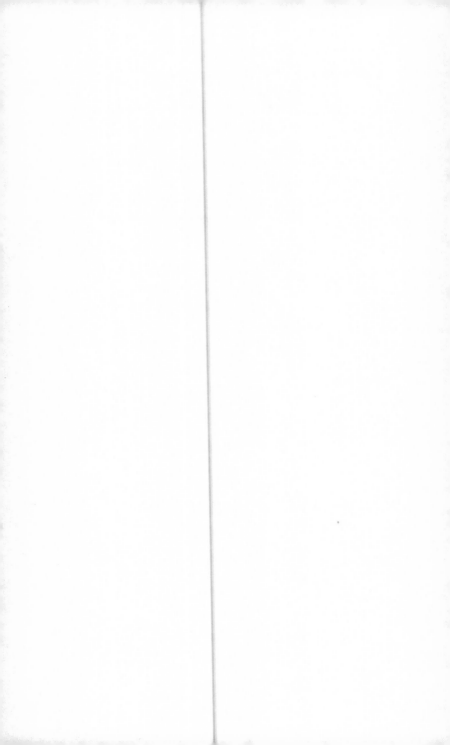

Made in the USA
Columbia, SC
16 April 2021